Pretty in Pink, Wicked with Spurs

Sugar Lee Ryder

PRETTY IN PINK, WICKED WITH SPURS

Copyright © 2012 by Sugar Lee Ryder

ISBN-13: 978-1479140558

ISBN-10: 1479140554

Paperback Edition printed in the United States and published by Banty Hen Publishing in conjunction with Glair Publishing, September 2012.

For more about Banty Hen Publishing, please visit:
www.bantyhenpublishing.com.

For more about Glair Publishing, please visit:
www.glairpublishing.com.

Other Books by Sugar Lee Ryder

Sagebrush and Lace

Six guns, whips and wild, wild women!

1876: Time to throw away the corsets
and draw down on the Old West.

When Horace Greeley said "Go West Young Man"
he never would have thought that two young women
would take his advice to heart. Striking out against all
odds and risking everything to be together.

Society calls them Sapphists.
Chief Sitting Bull calls them 'Big Magic'.
Buffalo Bill Cody and Wild Bill Hickok
call them friends.
Pinkerton's detectives want them alive.
Clarke Quantrill's gang of outlaws want them dead.

Two runaway women in a man's world
risk their very lives to be together.

See the full listing of J.D. Cutler
and Sugar Lee Ryder's works at:

www.JDCutler.com
~and~
www.SugarLeeRyder.com

Other Books from Banty Hen Publishing

Cowgirl Up

Part One of the 'Cowgirl Up' Trilogy
A hot romance with a young, independent
ranch woman that meets her match in this
novella about bulls, rodeo cowboys
and the difference between sex and love.

See the full listing of Sugar Lee Ryder's works at:
www.SugarLeeRyder

The Adventures of Amanda Love

Firefly meets *Flash Gordon* as con-artist and adventurer Amanda
Love travels the star systems of the frontier. Her ample charms
include the bluest eyes west of Delta Vega, and a body that could
give a pious man a wet dream in a skin-tight spacesuit.

She and her crew of loyal misfits take their traveling 'pay to pray'
Salvation Show out to the lonely, backwater alien planets that
dot fringe space. But her latest con nearly becomes her last,
when she and her crew are attacked by Malco Trent, the man
who runs the galaxy's most corrupt company: Mal Corp.

See the full listing of Michael Angel
and Devlin Church's works at:

www.MichaelAngelWriter
~and~
www.DevlinChurch.com

FOREWORD FOR
PRETTY IN PINK,
WICKED WITH SPURS

When I first wrote *Cowgirl Up*, it was a short
story that turned into a novelette. After publishing,
it garnered enough interest that a paperback
was released. Then an audio book.

Pretty In Pink, Wicked With Spurs is the second
book in a trilogy about Honey Durbin and the
Double D ranch. The third novelette, Who Left
the Gate Open will be the third and final part
in the story of Honey Durbin, J.D. Colby, and
the Double D ranch.

Oh, and don't forget Nero Junior!

ACKNOWLEDGMENTS

I wish to acknowledge the staff at
Glair Publishing for all their hard work!

DEDICATION

To all the cowboys that ride the bulls and provide endless entertainment for their audience - at the cost of their broken bones, all for a silver belt buckle.

A special dedication to the bulls. These majestic animals undoubtedly have the best sense of humor of God's creatures. Exercised at the expense of the cowboys that try to better them.

I swear I can hear them laughing as they do a victory lap around the arena with the rodeo clowns and the ring men trailing behind.

CHAPTER ONE

Insistent, heavy fists pounded on the door. I jerked to semi-consciousness out of a sound sleep. Before I could clear my head from the cobwebs of slumber I heard the urgent and raucous beating of the barnyard triangle, 'Clang! Clang! Get up! Get up! There's trouble!'

The clanging and pounding on the door grew more persistent as I shook my head to try and stir up the thinking process. Through the barrage of pounding I could hear someone yelling. *"Fire!"*

I jumped out of bed and threw on my robe and quickly cinched up the waist and hurried to the living room. Juana had just gotten to the door a few seconds before me, her face ashen as she jerked the door open. Sam stood on the porch leaning on one arm against the door jamb, out of breath, his nightshirt hastily shoved into his pants, its tail hanging out of the top.

I stepped through the doorway and looked beyond him at a red and orange glow that filled and lit the night sky with a hideous glare. I could see the silhouettes of the ranch hands as they scurried about in pandemonium. They had grabbed up hoses, buckets and shovels, anything that could be grabbed and used to fight fire with. They rushed toward the barn.

Juana stood transfixed with her hand up to her mouth, as with the other hand she crossed herself. "Madre de Dios!"

I turned back into the house and almost tripped over Daddy Buck who had come out of his room in his wheel chair to find out what all the ruckus was about.

"Daddy! The barn's on fire!"

A look of anguished disbelief took over the sleep-fogged face. I pushed past him and grabbed up the telephone and dialed 911. The operator picked up after two rings.

"This is Honey Durbin at the Durbin Ranch out on Highway 38. We need a fire truck right away." After I gave the operator the required information I hung up the phone, turned to my father. "You stay here in the house! You won't be any help out there, and I cain't worry about you right now." I pushed past him and ran to my room to put on some clothes.

By the time I got out of the house and over to the barn I saw J.D.'s fire-lit body against the bright backdrop. The ranch hands were losing the battle and I could hear the panicked stock inside the barn. J.D. had already started to open up the barn doors as I ran to the barn's hitching rail and grabbed a couple of saddle blankets that hung there and threw one to J.D.. He instantly knew what I wanted and he threw the saddle blanket over his head like a magic cape and opened the barn door.

I hollered over to one of the ranch hands who had been using the hose.

"Wet us down!"

The draft from the open door caused the burning bits of hay from the hay mow to swirl down and around the frightened horses' heads. They reared and kicked in their stalls. Embers fell onto the wet saddle blankets. They were all that protected J.D. and me as we made our way to the maddened and frenzied animals. We hurried through the barn and opened the gates to the stalls to let the horses out.

The animals wouldn't leave.

Amid their flaying hooves J.D. and I tried to get a hold of the horses' halters. J. D. quickly grabbed up two of the wipe-down cloths and threw one to me. We barely had time to cover the eyes of the terrified equines to lead them to safety. Once the first two horses were led out, the others followed out the barn door. Once out and they saw the safety of the night, they took off running. A couple of ranch hands almost got trampled on as they tried to grab the fleeing, terrified animals.

"Let 'em go, we'll collect them later!" I screamed over the din caused by the frantic whinnying and the roar of the fire storm that the dry hay and old wood of the barn fueled.

Sooty sweat ran down my neck. I could feel the grittiness as it left black streaks down my neck and chest. I threw off the sodden saddle blanket. I could see steamy smoke rise from the burnt holes along it.

I looked over at J.D. His shoulders had burn marks on them. "You alright?"

"Yeah." As J.D. spoke, the huge rafters of the barn caved in. The swoosh of hot wind formed from its collapse as it belched out with its breath of brimstone caused us and the other ranch hands to fall back from the force of the inferno. It looked like the very gates of hell had opened up.

The roar of the flames and the caved-in ceiling caused the cattle in the pens next to the barn to panic, and they surged against the fence and brought it down. Fear transformed the small herd into a stampeding tsunami of flesh.

Once out, they scattered, further confused by the fire trucks that came through the ranch gates with lights blazing and sirens blasting.

The tank trucks pulled into the yard, and the cattle and horses dodged them. By the time the firemen were able to get the water going, the barn had become totally engulfed in the hungry flames. The best they could do was keep the rest of the out-buildings from going up in smoke with it. J.D. and I walked to the porch to join Buck, Juana and Sam. We all watched in fascinated horror as the building was consumed.

I looked at J.D. and the men of the Double D, then spoke to Juana. My voice was raspy from the smoke that filled the air.

"Juana, would you make some coffee please. We're going to be needing it." I sighed as I looked at the chaos of the barn yard. "Lots of it."

Tiredly I sat down on the front steps and wrapped my arms around Daddy Buck's legs and laid my head against the side of his knee and watched. I told myself that the tears in my eyes were from the smoke, while the scene played out before me, a good representation of what I imagined hell would look like.

J.D. went to join the rest of the ranch hands to gather the herd of milling cattle and horses and put them into the pasture. It took until dawn before the firemen could get all the hotspots out, and the ranch hands to get the animals rounded up.

Meanwhile Juana made me get up and gave directions to me to help set up an outside kitchen. She had gallons of coffee, steaming hot, and steak and potatoes frying on the grill. She seemed to know what would be needed by us all.

While the firemen packed up their gear and made ready to leave, the Fire Chief came up to Daddy Buck.

"You Mr. Durbin?"

"Yes. I am. I must say you and your boys did a fine job. A damn fine job. I'm not sure what else would have been lost if you guys hadn't made it out here when you did."

"Thank you for the kind words. I am Fire Captain Sean McDougal, and I need to talk with you a minute about the fire."

"Why sure. I don't really know anything about it other than I was woke out of my sleep."

I walked up to the two men and stood quiet and listened to what the Chief had to say.

The fireman held a can with a nozzle on it. It was charred and twisted, but I still could distinguish it. A gasoline can. Buck looked down at it.

"What've you got there, Chief?'

"I was about to ask you if it had been policy to store gasoline in the loft of your barn?"

"Why, that would be real stupid, now wouldn't it?"

"That's what I think. Well, we found this laying in the rubble. From its position in the rubble it seemed to have been in the loft. It kind of looks to me like someone actually *wanted* to burn your barn down."

CHAPTER TWO

"Damn idiots!" The first words spat out of my mouth as I stomped into the house. Daddy Buck looked up at me and J.D. as we came into the living room. I slammed the door behind me.

"Those damn idiots at the insurance company are saying that there's evidence that the barn fire had been set. Well duh!" I slumped down onto the couch and leaned back into it. J.D. came in and sat down next to Daddy Buck.

"They're saying that there will be no payment to replace the barn and the equipment that was lost until the person or persons are caught."

"Well, Honey darlin', I cain't say as how I disagree with them about it bein' set. But them not paying, that don't seem right. I looked at the policy and it don't say anything like that in it."

I put my hands up to my face and covered my eyes for just a minute. Wiped them down my cheeks and said. "No, Daddy, it doesn't, exceptin' if they think that the insured property owner is at fault."

I couldn't bear to look at Daddy. I didn't need to see what I knew was there. His silence in response said it all. I continued. "A Jack Hunnicut, their insurance investigator, will be out here sometime tomorra' to go over the remnants of the barn and to get a statement from us before the official hearing."

Daddy's voice sounded small. "A hearing?"

"Yeah, Daddy. A hearing. The investigator will be comin' out to investigate. He will determine if there will be charges of arson placed against us."

The ensuing silence that followed my last statement was broken by a rapping sound on the front door jamb. It announced the arrival of Sam. I caught sight of him out of the corner of my eye and waved my hand for him to come in. He pulled open the screen door and with his hat in his hand he approached the three of us as we sat around the living room hearth.

"Miss Honey. I saw that you had come back from town. What did the insurance company say?"

"They're thinking about bringing an arson charge against us. They think they have evidence that we set fire to our own barn for the insurance money."

I could see the look on Daddy's face as I said those words. Daddy had worked hard all his life and he was as honest as they come. Last year hadn't been easy, with money being so tight an all. But the Double D was making it just fine. The fact that anyone would even suspect him of anything underhanded was devastating to him. My heart gave a twinge.

Daddy Buck didn't say anything more; he just turned his wheel chair around and headed out of the room.

"Daddy? Where you goin'?"

He stopped and turned his head to me. "I need to go and think on this a spell. By myself." As he left the room J.D. laid his hand on my shoulder and gave it a squeeze. Sam just looked at me.

I said nothing.

Did nothing.

It felt as if the weight of the whole ranch had just descended onto my shoulders.

Sam shook his head, stared at the floor and put his hat back on. As he turned he mumbled out, "Let me know iffen there's anythin I can do, Miss Honey."

"I will, Sam. Just tell the boys not to touch anything that's around the barn. We have to leave it until the investigator arrives and is finished out there."

"Will do." With that said he left. I could hear his boots cross the porch.

I laid my head in J.D.'s lap, and he stroked my hair. "J.D., what are we gonna do?"

He sighed. "Well Honey, there ain't much to do until after we hear what the investigator has to say tomorrow. But whatever happens I want you to know I will be there for you. You just have to let me know."

* * *

Juana had breakfast ready and on the table when I got up. J.D. had already been sitting and waiting for me. With his hand around a cup of coffee, he stared into the cup. I shambled over, gave him a peck on the cheek and sat down.

"You're up early. How's your shoulders? They looked pretty raw last time I saw them." I reached over and lifted the collar edge of his shirt up to take a peek.

"Yeah, Sam and me had breakfast already. I'll live." He winced and I removed my hand. "Juana gave me some salve to put on them. Feels like I just stayed in the sun too long." He sipped his coffee.

"Sam and I needed to figure out how we're going manage the ranch until we replace some of the equipment and tack that was lost. I already sent Toby in town with Billy Bob to get some saddles and replacement gear so we can manage the ranch until we get everything all sorted out."

"Did the fire reach the feed barn? I didn't have the heart to go look, just yet."

"Naw. We were lucky with that. Thanks to the firemen none of the hay was even singed."

"That's good." I took a sip of my coffee and set the cup on the table. My fingers did a sort of circular dance around the cup as I stared down into the dark liquid. "J.D., there's something nigglin' at me."

"What is it, Honey?"

"Why didn't the fire extinguisher system go off?"

"What do you mean?"

"Sam had a fire extinguisher system put in the barn three years ago. Why didn't it go off? "

J.D. didn't say a word for a minute; he just looked at me with an unformed and un-answered question written across his face. He stood up and shoved his chair back to its place.

"Well, the way I figure, that will be something the insurance investigator will be looking into. I think he will be here pretty early this morning. The sooner he gets out here the less time we have to cover up any evidence."

I glared at him. "That's not funny, J.D."

"I'm sorry, Honey, I just tried to cheer you up a bit and did a really poor job of it."

He put his hand over mine and held it for a second, gave it a squeeze and let go when Juana refilled my cup of steaming liquid. I took a sip as J.D. left.

"Juana, is Daddy up yet?"

"No, querida. I looked in on him and he is still sleeping."

No sooner had she said that when around the corner of the living room wall came Daddy Buck hobbling along on his cane.

"No, damn it, I'm not still sleeping."

I could read the pain he was enduring by the grimace of his face, the puffing effort in his breath as he approached.

I stood up and went to him and gave him a kiss on his forehead. "Good morning, Daddy." I took his arm and helped him to his seat at the head of the table.

"Where's your wheelchair?"

"I ain't gonna meet with no insurance investigator with me sitting below him in a wheelchair. I want to face him eye to eye."

I could tell that Daddy had his hackles up. The implication from the Fire Chief the night before of his being behind the barn fire just made him plum mad.

"Well, he ought to be here anytime, so you best eat some breakfast."

Before he could stick a fork into the steak and eggs Juana had set before him, the crunching of the driveway gravel caught our attention. Our heads turned toward the front door. I got up and went to the window and peeked through it. "Well, it looks like we won't have to wait any longer. Mr. Hunnicut has arrived."

* * *

Outside in the barnyard J.D. and Sam stepped up to meet Mr. Hunnicut as he opened his truck door and stepped out. Sam extended his hand toward the investigator. "Mr. Hunnicut? I am Sam Pennyworth, consultant to the Double D." He pointed to J.D. "This here is J.D. Colby, Ranch Foreman."

J.D. extended his hand to Hunnicut. "I'm sorry to make your acquaintance under these circumstances, Mr. Hunnicut."

After the amenities had been taken care of, Jack Hunnicut spoke in a let's get on with it voice. "I would like to speak with the Double D's owners."

J.D. gestured with his arm for the investigator to follow him over to the house. I saw them approach through the window. J.D. first, the investigator second and Sam bringing up the tail end. I met them at the door. Hunnicut was a rather hawkish looking man. Thin and tall, his jeans and work shirt hung about his body as if he were more scarecrow than man. He wore heavy-soled work boots and a hard hat; he didn't remove it when he came into the house. His large beak of a nose stuck out from his face at a sharp angle. It had a crook in it; must've been broke at least once. His hair cropped short could barely be seen above ears that stuck out from his head as if he would be looking for a nearby airfield. All I could think of was Ichabod Crane. He held onto a battered old tool box. I must say that, even though he had been congenially friendly with J.D. and Sam, his face had a scowl on it like he had been sucking lemons.

Sam took the introductions upon himself. "Mr. Hunnicut, this here is Honey and Buck Durbin. They own the Double D."

Buck extended his hand. "Mr. Hunnicut."

I did the same.

Mr. Hunnicut didn't beat around the bush.

"Mr. Durbin, I spoke with Captain Sean McDougal over the telephone and he seems to think that the fire that destroyed your barn had been set on purpose. That is why I am here. To determine for the insurance company if that is indeed the case."

Ignored hands dropped. Daddy Buck leaned on his cane but managed to stand to his full height. "Mr. Hunnicut, I can assure you that we most likely want to get to the bottom of this whole affair much more than you do. We..." He made a motion with his hand to indicate me. "My daughter and I have much more at stake than you or your company has." I didn't say anything; I knew my daddy wouldn't take too kindly to my intervention just yet. "My daughter has already been down to the agency office and found out that they're tryin' to get away without paying by trying to imply that we set fire to our own barn." With that said,

Daddy pushed past us, his anger fueling the force of his determined lopsided and limping walk. We all trailed behind him as he led the way toward the burnt out ruin of what was left of the barn. A lump formed in my throat as I approached it for the first time since the night before.

Hunnicut looked for a likely place to set his tool box down and settled on an overturned crate. He looked up at Daddy Buck and me. "I think that you and Miss Durbin need to leave me to my work. Maybe Mr. Colby could stay and help me out?"

"I'd rather Sam stay," said J.D. "He knows more about the things you're likely to ask than me. I'm just relatively new here so if you please, can he be with us?"

Hunnicut looked at Sam. Studied him then nodded his head, then went back to pulling stuff out of his toolbox, and Daddy and me went back over to the front porch of the house. I could tell by the beads of sweat on Daddy Buck's forehead that he was havin' trouble with his breathin'. When we arrived I helped him up the front porch steps and yelled. "Juana! Get Daddy somethin' to drink."

He slumped down into his rockin' chair and leaned back and laid his head against the back of the rocker. His cheeks were flamin' hot and his forehead wet with sweat. He closed his eyes until Juana arrived with a glass of lemonade.

I lifted it to his lips. "Here, Daddy, take a sip and just relax a bit."

His eyes opened and his hand came up to take the glass from me. "I'll be alright, Honey." He took a sip and with tired eyes he watched as Jack Hunnicut prowled through the ruins of the ravaged barn. Every once in a while the man would stoop and pick something up and place it in a bag and write something on it. He brought out a camera and snapped what seemed an endless amount of pictures. Sam and J.D. followed along like a pair of baby ducks, answering questions as they were asked.

The whole process took a couple of hours, but me and Daddy Buck stayed on that front porch and watched every move, until Hunnicut closed up his toolbox and deposited it into his truck's cab along with numerous large bags before he came over to us on the porch. I stood up.

"Well, what did you find?"

"I can't tell you that right now, but you will be getting a notice of the hearing date soon."

With that bit of non-information he returned to his truck, got in and drove away. My attention jumped between the two men.

"Sam! J.D.! What did he find?"

J.D. spoke up. "Well, he did find out that the water had been shut off to disable the fire sprinkling system, and he found out that it was set using an accelerant like the gasoline from the can that Fire Chief McDougal found."

"Did he tell either of you anything?" My eyes darted to where Sam stood. "What about you, Sam?"

"Well, Miss Honey, him not sayin' anything spoke more than what he did say. I would think that they're going to press charges for arson against you and Buck."

I heard a glass crash to the porch floor I turned, and what I saw chilled my blood. Daddy Buck's hand had dropped over the side of his chair and the lemonade glass had crashed into shards at the foot of the rocking chair. His head had jerked back and to the side. His other hand clutched at his throat.

"Juana, call 911!" I screamed out the words.

J.D. and Sam helped me get him out of the rocker and onto the porch floor, his face the color of burned out ashes. J.D. checked his pulse and began to administer CPR. Sam held me tight to keep me out of the way. J.D. worked and worked until the paramedics arrived after what seemed to be hours.

I was near hysterics when the ambulance roared into the barnyard with sirens blasting. Dust settled around the vehicle as the two paramedics seemed to jump out almost before it had come to a full stop. They descended upon Daddy Buck and almost shoved J.D. out of the way.

All I could do was stand back. I barely breathed as I watched in disbelief. When they pronounced Daddy dead, I let out a scream and tore myself away from Sam and went to Daddy Buck and laid my head on his chest and cried. It took J.D and Sam both to lift me off him so that the Paramedics could put him on the gurney and into the back of the ambulance.

I felt numb and cold as they pulled the blanket up and over his face. When they closed the doors and started the engine I could feel a hole develop in my heart. I vaguely heard Juana in the background weeping and barely noticed that the ranch hands had gathered around, taking off their hats. When the ambulance's engines started and it drove out of the yard silently and down the long drive, even J.D.'s arm around me didn't staunch the chill.

CHAPTER THREE

J.D. drove me in to the Grey's Funeral Home. Daddy didn't need an autopsy because he had been under doctor's care. Dr. Jessop said that the whole arson thing and the extra stress of Daddy Buck when he had walked out to the burned barn had just been too much for 'em.

J.D. offered to help me with the funeral arrangements. "You know, Honey, I can help you out with all this."

I don't know just what I felt at that time. J.D. was trying to be kind and be there for me. I didn't want to share my grief with him.

"No thank you, J.D. Daddy Buck had always taught me that there were two things for sure that a person needed to do. You needed to learn to saddle your own horse and shoot your own dog." I straightened my shoulders up. "I do reckon this comes under that bit of advice."

We didn't say much after the arrangements were done and we drove back to the ranch. When I got there I climbed out of the truck. I didn't say anything to J.D. Just left him standing beside it as I walked out and across the pasture and under old Nero's tree where I used to play when I was just a snot-nosed kid.

When I reached the other side I snaked my way through the fence and crouched down on my heels to think about what had happened the last year and half.

The green of the pasture and the backdrop of the still-standing building showed white. The dusty smell of the cattle and the hay came to me on a slight breeze. It smelled more sweet than any expensive French perfume. For a moment I was lost in remembrances. Then the smell of burnt wood and ash broke into my revelry. It brought my mind back to the issue at hand. I got up, took a look around, dusted off my jeans and headed back to the house.

When I walked in the door, Juana took an envelope from her apron pocket and held it out to me. "Honey, a deputy was here while you were gone. He dropped this off for you. I don't think it is good news."

I took the envelope from her and ripped it open. Inside was a court summons. I let out a coarse chuckle, and said to no one, "I see they didn't waste no time."

* * *

Jack Hunnicut took the stand and addressed the courtroom. "The principal problem with the Durbin barn burning was to determine the origin, that is, the ignition source of the fire. Once I determined that, finding the origin without an accidental ignition source, and a burned gasoline can left at the scene led me to conclude that somebody must have placed some fuel at that origin and ignited it with an open flame."

Hunnicut shifted his seat and looked directly at Judge Gallows and continued.

"In addition to the gasoline can, it had been found that someone had turned off the water source to the fire extinguisher system that had been installed in the barn."

Judge Gallows queried, "Mr. Hunnicut, is there anything else that you would like to say at this time?"

"Well, your Honor, my testimony is all my opinion but in the absence of a positive laboratory report, I can only conclude that the fire was intentionally set using a flammable liquid."

Hunnicut turned to face the court room. I couldn't say or do anything but listen to what he had been saying. Only one thing had been running through my head: *Who?*

The hawkish man continued unemotionally in his response to the Judge.

"When the front barn door was opened, it created a flash-over, and the longer the fire was allowed to burn after flashover, the more damage was done. But it is my determination that the act of arson had been committed."

Judge Gallows determined that there was enough evidence to warrant a trial, and I would stand accused for arson. He didn't think that I was much of a flight risk so he released me on my own recognizance. I felt numb. That seemed to be my general state of being these days.

As J.D. and I drove home after the hearing I was the first to speak. "J.D. We need to call the wedding off."

He slammed on the brakes and pulled over to the side of the road and turned to me.

"Why? For God's sake, it ain't planned for a few months yet!"

"Well, J.D., with Daddy dying and the arson charges against me, I don't think the timing is all that good."

"Honey, everybody knows that we plan on getting married. It's not like this is something out of the wide blue sky."

"I just don't think that I can concentrate right now."

"But, Honey, I can help you better if I'm your husband. Don't ya think?"

"Damn it, J. D.! I need to find out who done this to the Durbin's. To the Double D. I intend on finding out who it is and bringing them down. Right now that is all I can think of."

"Honey, I know that we need to clear your name. And we will. I can help, really I can."

"It is settled! The wedding is off. I need to get the Durbin name cleared and get the ranch back on top."

"I didn't hear my name in there. Honey, where do I fit in with your priorities?" His voice sounded hurt.

I couldn't help how he felt. All I knew at that moment was I needed to clear my name, and I needed to not let my daddy's ranch go under.

"J.D., right now I'm not sure where you fit in."

With that last statement of mine he put the truck in gear and pulled back onto the road and headed for the ranch. Neither of us spoke the rest of the way.

CHAPTER FOUR

The funeral service had been small. Only a few very close friends and the Double D hands attended. It amazed me to realize that the people that we Durbins had done business with for years actually appeared to believe the story that they had heard about the arson charges. It was difficult for me to face them. I couldn't help thinking that they were all very relieved that it had been held as a private memorial.

A lot had happened in the two weeks that had gone by since the barn burnt down. The inquest did one thing. It released the site for cleaning away the debris. J.D. had been working his butt off each day with the boys, getting the grounds cleared. I hadn't spent much time with him since the funeral. I was working on figuring out who would have done such a thing and wranglin' with the insurance companies. It seemed there were at least two to deal with. Me being brought up on arson charges didn't help our case with them.

I was sitting at the desk when J. D. came in after a day's labor. He came over to me and bent down to give me a kiss.

He smelled of sweat and soot and his face had black streaks down it. I reached my hands up to fend him off. "Not now J.D. I'm busy. Besides you're all dirty and smell like a campfire."

"Well, what do you expect me to smell like? I've been workin' out there in that mess all day." He straightened up. "You have any new ideas as to who would want to cause the Double D trouble.?"

"No I don't! How's the cleanup coming?"

J.D. put his hands in his pockets. "It's comin' along just fine. Me and the boys have it almost finished. It would be nice if we could start work on new construction."

I rounded on J.D. with the pent up anger that had been boiling up inside me. "Yes, J.D., it would be nice. It would have been nice if Daddy hadn't died. It would have been nice if we hadn't had the accident last year that killed our prize breeding bull. It would have been nice if the barn hadn't burned down." I stood up and lashed out. "But you know what? It all did happen. It all did happen, and now I am facing a jail sentence and the loss of the Double D. And you know what else? I am facing it alone."

J.D. took his hands out of his pocket and let them drop down along side of his body. His voice sounded quiet. "Honey, you don't have to do anything by yourself. Let's get married like we planned and I can be more of a help for you. Right now it's limited what I can do for you." He started to reach for me.

I brushed his hand aside and looked at him with tears brimming in my eyes. "No, J.D., this is something I have to do. I have to clear the Durbin name. My name. I have to restore the Double D."

J.D. stepped back away from me. His eyes burned with hurt and frustration that I had put there. My words were spoken and meant. I felt that I had the weight of the ranch on my shoulders at that moment. It was my problem and I had to deal with it.

"J.D., I'm sorry, but this is not your problem. I will deal with it in my own way."

"Honey, you are not always right. But there are two theories on how to argue with a woman. Neither one works." He turned to leave but stopped at the doorway and turned. "I reckon that the wedding is off." With that said he left me standing there by the desk.

Juana came in. I am sure that she had heard everything. "Querida, are you alright?"

I went to her and folded my arms around her with my head on her shoulder and started to cry. She held me and patted my head. "Shhh, mi'ja. Todo está bien."

"No, Juana, everything is not okay. If I don't find out who burnt the barn I could go to jail. We could lose the Double D." I looked up into her wizened face and smelled the comforting smell of fresh baked bread, chili peppers, onions and the comfort of the kitchen on her. Everything that said home to me. She rocked me back and forth as she stroked my hair. For just a few moments I felt as if everything would be alright.

It was also in those few moments that I made a resolution that I would get past this. I would clear my name and restore the Double D's reputation.

I raised my head up and placed my hands on Juana's shoulders. "Juana, thank you. You are always there for me when I need you. What would I ever do without you?"

"Querida, please just be careful. I think that there is a very bad man involved with this."

"Yes Juana, I will be very careful. But sometimes a cowgirl has to do what a cowboy can't."

CHAPTER FIVE

I woke up to the sound of a truck door slamming the next morning and put on my robe and went out to the front porch. J.D.'s truck was parked in front of Sam's place. He and Sam were standing by the truck when I came out. J.D. had just thrown his bucking rig up into the back of the camper. I heard the clang of the bell that hung from the rope. Sam gave me a look that would look good on a bloodhound as he turned away and walked back into his house.

"J.D., what's going on?"

"I'm heading out. There don't seem to be nothing here for me. Your wants don't seem to have me in there anywhere. The cleanup is done; it's just waiting for new construction. Besides, it's getting time for the rodeo circuit to start up. I don't think I'm out of practice. Been keeping my hand in with the training of the bucking stock. Maybe I can fetch me a couple more buckles afore the season ends."

I felt a pang to my heart but all I could say was, "Well, J.D, if all you got is your eight seconds, don't even bother walking my way, cause I wanted you for a lifetime but right now I won't pay your stay."

"Well, Honey, I had planned on stayin' here at the ranch. But it seems you don't need me and I won't stay where I'm not needed. I love you, but you only love the Durbin name and the Double D. Not me. It has been a pleasure, Miss Durbin, but I got to be goin'."

He extended his hand. I ignored it because I was unable to respond. He withdrew his hand and shrugged. I can only guess that he took my inaction for not caring. Then he turned and got into the cab of his truck. As he fired up the engine, he tipped his hat and his last words were, "Tell the boys I'll be seeing them. I aim to be around for a while."

As he backed the camper around and out of the yard I was left standing there staring after him as the dust from the truck's tires kicked up around me. My robe's edges flapped in the breeze. I hadn't noticed Sam had come out of his house and stood next to me.

"Well, Miss Honey, what are we going to do now?"

I didn't answer him. I just turned and stalked off to the main house. My eyes burned with held-back tears, and my whole body ached with the pain of the hole in my heart that had opened when daddy died. Now it was being rendered and wrenched as if it was being dragged out of me.

I felt like I had been abandoned. Left to fend for myself. What had I done to merit the trouble that had been dumped squarely into my lap and taken up residence for the duration?

* * *

When I began to go out and deal with the merchants in town I found a whole different set of problems. The Double D had been doing business with the locals for years. Now all of a sudden I had to do business in cash. Mine and the Double D's credit all of a sudden were no good. None of them had the gumption to admit to me face to face that anything other than the economy was at fault. But I could tell from their actions and the scuttlebutt from the boys when they came back from the Stompin' Grounds Saloon. The rumors that had been going around town said that the Double D was in financial trouble and the barn was set fire to for the insurance money.

As my trial date grew nearer, I came to the conclusion that Sheriff Hobbs hadn't done much in the way of finding out who had really been at fault for the fire. If I were to clear my name it would be up to me.

I knew that Toby and Billy Bob felt a little uneasy at being asked to come up to the main house but I felt it would be more appropriate to ask them up. More private from the other hands. Not that I didn't trust the guys, but I knew that Toby and Billy Bob were loyal to the Double D, especially after last year's accident. We all pulled together on that one.

After the three of us were seated and Juana brought a couple of beers for the two men, I said, "You're old enough to drink now aren't you Toby?"

"Why, yes'm I am."

"How's everything goin'?"

Billy Bob spoke up. "Miss Honey, you didn't call us in here to go over how the work load is goin'. You got Sam for that." He sat back against the couch, his booted foot on top of his knee.

"You're right, Billy Bob, I didn't." I sat my beer down. "You boys still spend some time at the Stompin' Grounds?"

"Yeah, we do. Thar's nothin' or nowhere else really around here." Toby had always been ready to talk.

"You boys know what a jam I'm in right now, don't you?"

"Yes, Miss Honey, we do. I think I can speak for Toby here," Billy Bob pointed at Toby, "when I tell you that we stand behind you all the way. When we ride, we don't worry about the fall. It interferes with the ride."

"I am so glad to find that out because right now I need to have someone on my side." When I said that, the two men looked at one another, not understanding. "It has always amazed me what information could be found out at a bar. What I need you two to do is hang out at the Stompin' Ground and see what you can find out."

Billy Bob wanted to know what they were lookin' for in specifics.

"Well, I think that whoever set fire to the barn is from around here. Someone that holds a grudge against the Durbin's. I also think that it is likely that whoever it is will eventually shoot his mouth off." I let out a sigh. "I only hope that it is soon. My court date is coming up and I am pretty sure that the Sheriff is not giving this much of his time. If I am to have my name cleared I will have to do it myself."

We clinked our beers in agreement and drained the bottles.

As Toby and Billy Bob left I had to fight off the fear that maybe the persons or person responsible had left town and I would have to stand trial. A cold chill ran down my arms and up my back. I wished J.D. had been there.

* * *

21

Sam did a great job making do and getting the ranch work done though he missed having J.D. there to take care of the everyday chores of runnin' the ranch. I couldn't help him much because I needed to concentrate on my investigation. The only one that we'd had a run-in with recently had been Jake Tallmadge. I had fired him for going up against J.D.. *Surely he wouldn't be holding a grudge. I had paid him extra severance and given him a good reference.*

The more I thought about Jake, the more I began to wonder. He certainly knew the barn well enough and where the water cut-off to the fire extinguisher system was. He had been pretty steamed up about being let go.

It was about 10:30 PM when a knock on the door caused me to jump out of my musings. I went to the door and opened it. Toby and Billy Bob stood on the porch.

They took off their hats as I asked them in.

Billy Bob evidently was the decided spokesman for the two.

"Miss Honey, I am so glad that your light was on. We wanted to get home in time to tell you."

"Tell me what? Don't keep me in suspense."

"Well, we were hanging out at the bar like you said. Jake Tallmadge came in. He had been drinking afore he showed up, so he was already pretty drunk."

"Go on."

"He came in and ordered a drink. Said he was celebrating that the Durbins' were finally getting their due. He had seen to that."

I listened intently. "He actually said that out loud in the bar?"

"Yes'm he did. And he said that it was easy as turning off a water tap."

CHAPTER SIX

"Damn it, Sheriff Hobbs. There are three kinds of men in this world. The ones that learn by reading. The few who learn by observation. The rest of them have to pee on the electric fence themselves. Which one are you?"

"Miss Durbin, there is no need to get sarcastic. I'm just tellin' you that I can't go around arresting someone just because you say that he bragged about turning off a water tap after he'd been drinking in a bar."

"Sheriff, it isn't your ass that will be going to jail or your ranch that will be lost if we don't nail Jake Tallmadge."

"I know you have a lot at stake here. But you have to understand that I need something else to be able to just walk up and arrest someone for a crime of shootin' their mouth off. And right now that is all I've got."

Exasperated, I turned on my heels and stomped out of the sheriff's office. If I hadn't left I might have ended up in the hoosegow again. The truth of the matter was, the sheriff was right. I didn't have anything tangible on Jake. I drove home tiring my mind out wondering how I would be able to prove that it was Jake that had for some reason felt that he needed to get even with me and Daddy Buck. *He must have known what it could have done to my father. I couldn't understand his motivation. Buck Durbin had always been fair to his employees. And didn't I give him a fair severance check with a good recommendation?*

I turned the engine off and laid my head down onto my arms as they lay across the steering wheel. A shadow blocked out the sunlight coming in the window. It made a chill run down my spine and startled me. I hadn't heard anyone come up. I quickly turned my head, and saw John Twofeathers standing by the open driver's window.

"Honey, are you all right? I didn't mean to scare you."

I came out with a nervous little giggle. "Yeah, I'm okay, I just hadn't heard you come up. I've got a lot of stuff on my mind.

After all, you are an Indian and all." I tried to make light of my fright. "How ya doin'? When did you get back in town?"

John stepped back and opened the truck's door for me and offered his hand as I slid down out of the cab. I grabbed my stuff off the seat.

"Let's get in out of the sun and you can tell me whatcha been up to lately? How about some of Juana's fresh lemonade?"

"Sounds good, just lead the way." He stepped aside to let me lead the way into the house.

We sat in the living room with a glass of Juana's guaranteed-to-pick-your-spirits-up-or-you're-dead lemonade in our hands. I had to admit that it felt good to have someone sit there with me. Someone that I trusted and could be honest with.

"So, John, when did you get back in town and where you workin' at?"

"I got back into town just about a week before your barn burnt down."

"I didn't see you at Daddy Buck's funeral."

"It was hard not to attend. But I thought that maybe it was better for me to stay away, seems you had enough on your hands at the time. Besides, you had J.D. there. I didn't figure it would be appropriate."

John took a sip of his lemonade and smacked his lips. "What does Juana put in this to make it taste so good?"

"I think it has a little bit of white rum. I'm not really sure, the only thing is I wouldn't drive after more than two if I were you."

He set it down and leaned back into the sofa, and looked me straight in the eyes. "How are things goin' with you? For real."

I leaned back and put my foot up under me and ran my fingers through my hair to gain time before answering him. I decided to be candid.

"Not so good, John. The wedding is off and J.D. has left the ranch. I have reason to believe that it was Jake Tallmadge that set fire to the barn but I ain't got nothin' except that, a suspicion, and my trial date is coming up faster than I care to even think about. So I'm not doin' so good right now."

John opened his arms. "Come here, Honey."

I didn't hesitate. It felt good to just melt into his strong arms. I don't know why but I started to cry. We sat there for a long while until I got it all out. He just held me and let me get it all out.

Embarrassed, I sat up. "I'm sorry, John."

"No need to be. What are friends for if you can't lean on them once in a while?"

I wiped my face with the back of my hand and took a sip of lemonade.

"John, how come you are here anyway?"

"Well, Honey, I came to see how you were doin' and I think I have some information for you that may be of interest."

"Don't just sit there! Tell me!"

"I came back in town about a week before your barn burnt down and took a wrangler job over at Chisholm's. Jake Tallmadge had already been workin' there. Ever since you let him go, I believe." He paused.

"Go on, John. For heaven's sake, go on."

"Well, right off he would bad mouth the Double D to anybody that'd listen. Course, most didn't. That very thing seemed to rankle him the most. He couldn't get no sympathy from anybody. They all just thought that it was sour grapes on account of J.D. comin' in and getting the girl and the ranch so to speak."

My face reddened a little at that, remembering how John had been involved and all.

"Anyway he came in from the Stompin' Grounds last night and had a snoot full. He was stumbling blind drunk and woke up most of the guys in the bunk house. He was a muttering to himself about how he showed the high and mighty Durbins. Then I saw him take out a piece of feed sack with something wrapped inside of it. I watched as he unwrapped a silver belt buckle."

"What does a silver belt buckle have to do with the barn burning down?"

"When he passed out it was laying in his hand and I went over and looked at it. That buckle was for a World

Championship Bull rider. My guess was that buckle belonged to J.D."

"J.D. never did find it in the burnt-out rubble. He had put all of his trophies in the tack room, including the buckle. There was so much that had been destroyed he just figured it had been also. But if Jake has it then that means he must have taken it as a souvenir."

I flung my arms around John's neck and gave him a big kiss. "Oh, John, I love you!"

"I only wish you did, Honey. I only wish you did."

I looked at John sitting there. A little part of me wished I did also.

"John, will you tell this to Sheriff Hobbs?"

"Yes, Honey, I will be glad to."

Feeling the best I had in a very long time, I got up and went to the phone, punched in the numbers. It rang twice. "Hello, Sheriff Hobbs? This is Honey Durbin. I just might have enough for that warrant."

There was a pause.

"What have you got, Miss Durbin?"

"I have an eye witness to evidence that Jake Tallmadge was at the ranch the night of the fire. My witness also heard him threaten to get even with me and Daddy Buck for firing him."

"Who is this witness, Miss Honey?"

"It's John Twofeathers, he is a wrangler for Chisholm's. He has been working with Jake since about a week before the fire. He is willing and able to testify."

"Can John Twofeathers come in right away to sign a statement?"

"Sheriff, we are on our way as we speak."

I hung up the phone and motioned for John to come with me as I almost ran out of the door. I shouted, "Juana, I'll be back soon! Tell Sam that I am at Sheriff Hobbs's office." The door slammed behind us.

It took about a century to get an arrest warrant out of old Judge Gallows and another decade to get out to the Chisholm Ranch.

Sheriff Hobbs wasn't none too happy about me wanting to follow him out to the ranch, but as determined as I was he relented finally and a small entourage arrived together. The ranch hands seeing the Sheriff's 4x4 gathered around the vehicles when we drove up. We parked out front of the bunkhouse. Mr. Chisholm came out of his house to greet us.

He was soft spoken with a voice that told me he wasn't the kind of man that anyone wanted to ever cross. He shook hands with Sheriff Hobbs as the sheriff explained why we were there. He pulled the warrant out of his shirt pocket and handed it to Mr. Chisholm.

Chisholm opened the piece of paper and as he read it his face grew dark as if a thunder storm lay brewing under his sun-tanned face. His voice sounded a rich baritone when he looked out at the faces of his ranch hands. "Any of you boys know where Jake's at?"

One of the ranch hands stepped up. He looked at Sheriff Hobbs sheepishly. "Last time I saw Jake he was over in the bunk house."

Chisholm spoke; I could tell by his tone he wasn't happy. "When was that?"

"About a hour ago." He looked around at the others.

"You boys got nothin' to do round here?"

They all scattered like cockroaches when the kitchen light was turned on as he motioned toward the bunk house and led the way for our little posse. He shoved the door open and it banged into the wall. Jake wasn't there.

CHAPTER SEVEN

Sheriff Hobbs did some asking around the Chisholm ranch to see if there was anything he could learn about Jake, while John and I went back to the Double D. John had to pick up his truck and I needed to make a call to the insurance company. With the charges dropped against me the insurance had no choice but to pay up.

I had asked John to stay for dinner so we could get caught up on everything else that had been going on in each other's life. John was turning out to be a real good friend. He didn't stay too late; daylight comes early for the wrangler. It's up before daylight to get the horses fed while you get your rig together. Eat breakfast then set about your chores for the day's wages. Chisholm's was a working cattle ranch, not a specialty ranch like the Double D. I smiled to myself. *Even in this modern time the cowboy still needs to be up before sun up.*

As I lay in my bed I realized how quiet the house was and that I felt lonely in my bed. I missed J.D. and tomorrow I had to lock horns with the insurance company and then see what I could do to salvage the rodeo season's stock requirements. With the arson charges against me, I couldn't get anyone to deal with the Double D. Now that they had been dropped...

But it was late in the season.

"Daddy Buck, if you can hear me, please help and let me know what to do." I closed my eyes to shut out the darkness of my room and drifted off to sleep.

The next morning I was up and at the breakfast table planning my day when Juana let Sam in. He came over to the table with his hat in his hand. "Mornin', Honey."

"Mornin', Sam. Have a seat and some coffee. You have breakfast yet? Juana is doin' flapjacks this morning."

"Naw, Honey, as much as I like her flapjacks. I already had breakfast 'bout two hours ago."

Sam shot Juana a smile. I swear she blushed.

"Okay, Sam, what do you need this morning?"

"I was just wonderin' what's going on with everything. You know, the barn and all. The fellas are gettin' kind of worried. They ain't seen no sign that we're rebuildin', and I don't know what to tell 'em."

"Well, Sam, you tell 'em that the Double D ain't licked yet. The arson charges have been dropped and I am going to the insurance office today."

His smile lit up his whole face like it was Christmas morning.

"Does that mean we can start rebuildin'?"

"I believe it does."

"You said the charges have been dropped? Well, what changed their minds?"

"John Twofeathers heard and saw Jake Tallmadge had J.D.'s silver buckle from the trophy room."

"Really?"

"Yep, it was enough for Sheriff Hobbs to get off his butt and get a warrant for Jake."

"Well, don't that beat all? Was there an arrest?"

"Nope! When we all got out to Chisholm's, Jake had pulled up stakes and left without tellin' anybody he was goin', didn't even stop to collect his pay. I'd say that's the actions of a guilty man."

"If you excuse me, Honey, I got to go tell all the men." He started to leave.

"Ah, Sam."

He hesitated. "Yes'm."

"Please tell Toby and Billy Bob that they were right. It was Jake."

Sam smiled, put on his hat and went out to tell the boys that we would be rebuilding soon, that everything was going to be fine.

I didn't have the heart to tell him that nothing had been settled yet. Just that I wouldn't be going to jail. At least not until I caught up to Jake Tallmadge.

* * *

The meeting with the insurance company went a lot better than I had anticipated. There were just a couple of formalities and a whole lot of paperwork to get through but that was pretty much all there was to it. It was about time something went well for the Double D. I made arrangements for the money to be wired to the Double D bank account that afternoon.

As well as it went with the insurance company things went bad real quick. I gave a couple of phone calls to the stock procurers for the rodeos around the regular circuit, and as I had feared they had found suppliers for all their needs for bucking bulls. It was nice to hear that they liked the Double D stock better, but since they hadn't heard from us they had had to make sure they weren't caught up short.

I pulled into the local rodeo grounds and as the dust settled around my Big Red, Mr. Pickett came hobbling out.

"Honey! I been wonderin' where you been, girl."

I got down out of the truck.

"How you doin', Mr. Pickett?"

"I'm doing just fine. Although I'm not so sure that I'd say the same about the looks of you. You look like you've lost some weight."

"Mr. Pickett, have you made contract with any bucking bull providers yet?"

"You get right to the point, don'tcha, girl?"

"Well I've been to all the others; they all've gone to some other ranch. They said they hadn't heard from the Double D, couldn't wait any longer."

"I'm glad you came to me. A couple more days and I'd have done the same as the others. I wouldn't have had a choice. But here you are so let's deal."

I drove slower than normal back to the Double D, my mind on a lot of things. With only one contract for the season money would be very tight. The insurance money had to go to the reconstruction and new equipment or we wouldn't be able to operate at all. But once that was gone...

The dirt crunched and crackled as I drove into the yard at the ranch. I saw Sam over with the boys; they had a couple of the pregnant cows in the small pen with a chute at one end, to give them their prenatal check. As I got out of the truck I had an idea that might just get us through this whole mess.

Sam looked up as I approached. "Afternoon, Miz Durbin." That was Sam, very formal whenever he was out with the hands. He always told me that he didn't want them gettin' any funny ideas about familiarity, wanted them to remember they was hired hands.

"Afternoon, Sam. How's everything goin'" I nodded toward the cows.

He picked up a towel and wiped his hands as he came over to the fence where I leaned up against it, propping one foot on the bottom rail.

"Well, the cows are doing fine. Then of course, they are Double D cows."

I looked over the small herd in the corral. They were all fat, sleek and prime stock. Just how Daddy Buck had always dreamed. Sam had taken a personal pride in them, seeing as how it was his breeding program that produced them.

"Sam, how many pregnant cows we got right now?"

"We got twenty confirmed took. Maybe five more not sure. Need the vet to come out and check 'em, I cain't tell."

"Why, Sam! I never thought that you'd ever say there was something you couldn't do where a Brahma was concerned."

Sam blushed, then came back with, "Well, females of any kind always did confuse me a bit."

He grabbed the top rail, climbed over and stood beside me. "Let's go on over to the porch, Miss Honey, you look like you got somethin' to tell me."

"Indeed I do, Sam, indeed I do."

I poked my head into the house and asked Juana to bring out some lemonade then sat in one of the rockin' chairs with Sam sittin' next to me. By the way he was leaning forward I could tell he was anxious to hear what I had to say. I knew it and wanted to savor the good news so I waited until Juana brought our drinks. I took a sip. I could see Sam was about to jump out of his skin.

"The insurance released the money." I said it as calmly as I could.

"Yippee!"

He yelled so loud the guys at the cow's pen turned to look to see what the hell was goin' on.

"Now, Honey, you're not kiddin' an old man, are ya?'

"Nope! The money is already in the bank."

I could see the wheels turning in his head.

"Well, don't get too excited, Sam."

He looked at me. "Somethin' else and it ain't good."

"You're right about that. We only got one contract to supply stock to. Pickett's the only one. And if I had gotten to him any later we wouldn't have him."

Sam pushed his hat back on his head. "Damn! That's not good."

"No, it's not, but I think if we sell some of the stock off we might pull through. You know, at least for the next year or so. Get back on our feet."

"That's why you asked about the cows?"

"You got it. I figure that we can hold an auction and sell off half the pregnant cows and a few of the yearling bulls. That should get us... oh, maybe a hundred thousand dollars or so. With Nero's blood runnin' in their veins I'm sure of it."

Sam mused out loud. "With the bunch of two and four year olds, we could just make a good comeback next year. Get our bids out early. Yeah, it might just work out."

"That's what I thought. And it will give us time to get the barn built."

"Yes'm it will. I got to go tell the boys." He stood up and started to step down off the porch to go back to work and hesitated. "Ah, Honey, is there any chance that J.D. will be coming back? I could sure use his help about now."

I looked down at my hands as I answered him. "I don't know, Sam. I just don't know right now."

CHAPTER EIGHT

The barn's construction had gotten under way so the paddock pen was usable and would be where the stock would be brought into for the potential buyers to examine them before they went up on the sale block. It was mid-summer so it was hot and muggy. We set up a canopy and platform high up enough for the auctioneer to look down at the stock and people. There was another canopy in the barnyard where we offered water and sodas for buyers.

About an hour before the sale was to start the yard filled up with trucks and trailers. Auction day. It was always exciting, and created the impression of being at a country fair. It gave all the good ole boys a chance to come out and see how everyone else was doin', get caught up, and hopefully get a good deal.

The auctioneer had come out early in the morning to look over what the Double D had to offer.

"You got some prime stock here, Miss Durbin. The pedigree on them cows and the certificate of pregnancy should make for a good sale day." He took his handkerchief out of his pocket, took off his hat and mopped at his bald head.

In my answer to him I tried to sound positive with no feeling of desperation in my voice. "Well, I sure hope so."

I made my rounds and made small talk to all the ranchers. They gave me their condolences for Daddy Buck, and in the same breath they expressed their admiration for me, a little woman taking on such a big burden. Some of them made remarks about how they'd of thought I'd be married by now.

I gritted my teeth and smiled, while I tried to remember they meant well and just didn't know no better. Besides, I needed their money.

My heart skipped a beat when I saw a familiar old truck with a camper shell on it.

J.D.

I quickly searched the crowd to see where he might be. He was standing next to Sam over at the holding pen. But before I could get there the gavel hit the box that had been set up as a podium for the auctioneer. The loud CRACK! sounded like a gun shot, getting everyone's attention and announcing the beginning of the sale.

Everyone gathered around the narrow metal pipe corral run that had been set up for the cattle to be brought through one at a time. Toby and Billy Bob operated the gate at the incoming end of the run. A couple of the other boys operated the exit. J.D. and Sam stood next to the auctioneer on the raised platform to watch for bidders.

The first cow was ushered into the run. "Gentlemen, we are here today to sell these fine specimens of the Brahman breed. I don't need to tell ya'll about the reputation of the Double D for outstanding rodeo stock. What I will tell you is that every cow for sale here today is carryin' the calf of Nero, that fine bull that won five years in a row the Bucking Bull of the Year award. Every one of these cows has been certified to be healthy and pregnant. There is a certificate that has been notarized that each one has been artificially inseminated with Nero's sperm. Bidding will be in increments of five hundred dollars."

The first cow stood in the middle of the ring and stared out at all the men. Her big beautiful brown eyes looked at them. Her skin was sleek and had a sheen of health over the taut dun-colored skin. She snorted and blew out her breath, showing the disdain of royalty for the commoners that stood beyond the fence, when the auctioneer started his patter.

"Who'll give me five thousand dollars, for this beautiful cow?" He looked around and a man off to the side raised his hand. Sam hollered. "Yep!" and the auctioneer took it from there. "I've got five thousand, who'll give fifty-five hundred," and so it went until it topped out at twenty thousand dollars. The auctioneer looked over at me and I nodded my head yes. "I've got twenty thousand, anymore? Twenty thousand going once. Twenty thousand dollars, folks, for this fine cow. She's a carryin' a champion." The auctioneer waited a couple of seconds. "That's twenty thousand twice." Sam, J.D. and the auctioneer all looked around. "Last call! Sold! For twenty thousand dollars." The gavel came down at twenty thousand. About fifteen thousand light at what she had been worth.

And so it went with the rest of the stock. By the end of the day after giving the auctioneer his ten percent I was drained of energy and ideas. We had made less than half of what I had hoped for. As the trucks filed out of the yard I sat on the porch and watched the dust clouds as they whirled up behind the vehicles. I sat there thinking that I had never felt so tired, and alone. I sipped on beer and leaned back against the porch column and closed my eyes.

"Honey."

I opened my eyes to just a slit. I could see it was J.D. "Yes."

"Honey, can I talk to you a minute?"

I sat up and opened my eyes. "Sure, J.D.. How you been?"

"I've been better."

"Sit down, J.D., talk to me." I handed him a beer from the ice bucket I had sitting beside me. He took it and twisted the top off it and took a slug as he sat down.

"Well, J.D., what did you want to talk about?"

"Sam said he could use me around here."

"Oh, he did, did he?"

"He said it was up to you, if you wanted me to come back. He also said you found out that it was Jake that set the barn on fire."

"Sam is a regular old chatterbox, isn't he? What else did he tell you?"

"Nothin', he just said I should come and talk to you."

I took a drink. "Well, what he didn't tell you is that Jake has your Championship belt buckle which proves that he was here the night of the fire. And when the Sheriff went out to talk to him about it, he had packed up and left without telling a soul."

"How did you find out about it?"

"Well, Toby and Billy Bob had been the first to suspect him. They told me that Jake had been at the Stomping Grounds drunk on his ass and was shootin' his mouth off about us Durbins getting what we deserved and stuff like that. Well, it turns out that John Twofeathers had been hired on at the Chisholm's a couple of weeks before and was awake when Jake came in stumblin' drunk. John didn't like him so he just watched. His rule is to never approach a bull from the front, a horse from the rear, and never a fool from any direction, so he just waited until Jake passed out. Jake had been looking at something shiny before he passed out cold to the world. John went to see what he had been looking at."

"What was it?"

"It was a shiny silver belt buckle. A World Championship belt buckle... The belt buckle that you had in the trophy room with all your other trophies that we thought had been destroyed in the fire."

"Jake! That does make sense. Where is he now?"

"Well, Sheriff Hobbs thought so also. He went to Judge Gallows who issued the warrant for his arrest. When Hobbs went out to arrest Jake he had packed up and left. Didn't even collect his back pay."

"Whew! That was a tough break."

I looked at J.D. He hadn't changed much in the month that he'd been gone. I don't know what I expected. Maybe for him to grow two heads or somethin'. He had lost a little weight. Just goes to show how men seem to lose pounds when they don't get home cookin' and lovin'. Hells bells, I'd lost a few pounds myself. He sat there on the porch, not sayin' anything. All I could think of was how I needed him right then. Sam needed the help. Most of all, the ranch needed him if it was to recover. I leaned forward.

"J.D.?"

"Yes."

"J.D. Have you missed me at all?" I reached my hand over and placed it on his thigh. I felt a quiver go through him. That told me, yeah, he had missed me.

He looked down at his hands holding onto the beer. He swallowed hard, almost like he was embarrassed for the betrayal of his body's response to my touch.

He spoke, almost a whisper. "I missed you, Honey."

I slipped off the step, took his beer away from him and slid into his arms. I ran my hands up his chest and over and around his neck, pulled his face to mine and gave him a deep kiss. His arms came up and surrounded my body as he returned the kiss with a fever and passion and want.

The Oklahoma night sky overhead shone bright like diamonds spread out on a black piece of velvet. I pushed back away from his embrace, caught my breath and stood up. I reached my hand out and took his hand in mine.

"Come with me, J.D."

He didn't say anything as he rose up and followed me into the house. I didn't stop but continued into my bedroom. J.D. followed. When we were in the room I closed the door and began to undress him. I kissed each part of him that I laid bare. Then as he stood there in the moonlight, I undressed for him. Making sure that each piece of clothing I took off served to entice him. I could see the effect I had on him. His cock stood at attention. I came to him and rubbed my hand up and down his magnificent shaft. I knelt down in front of him and took him into my mouth. With my left hand I caressed his balls as my mouth worked up and down on him. My right hand followed the rhythm of my mouth as it pumped. I could feel the tightness start to build in him. I stopped and stood up and pulled him over to my bed.

I spread my legs and he entered me. He came within seconds. I could tell it embarrassed him that he had been so quick. What it told me was that he hadn't had any other woman since he left me. I curled up in his arms and snuggled down. My last thoughts before I drifted off to sleep traveled to the ranch and what needed to be done. And now I had J.D. to help me. The Double D would recover. I'd just made sure of that.

CHAPTER NINE

Sam sipped at his coffee. The Double D day always started early and at the breakfast table, where almost all the decisions had been made over the years. The antique, carved wooden table of the dining room was my mother's only extravagance. I didn't see any reason that ritual should end with Daddy Buck's death. Only now I sat at the head of the table. I didn't want the responsibility, but I didn't have any say in that.

J.D. joined us at the table.

"Mornin', Sam."

Sam looked at him and then me. Didn't say anything except, "Morning, J.D. Nice to see you here."

I finished my mouthful of egg and mopped at my lips before speaking. "Sam, J.D. has agreed to come back to the Double D."

"Well, Miss Honey, I kinda' guessed at that, seein' him here and all."

"I want him to take up the foreman's job again like he had been doing before he left."

"Yes'm, that'd be a good idea. He can ramrod the boys. The construction crews will be here the end of the week to get started on the new barn."

"Sam, I want you to tell all the men that J.D. will be taking over for you just like he done before. That okay with you?"

"It sure is, I was gettin' plumb tuckered out." He reached over and slapped J.D. on the shoulder. "Welcome back, son!"

J.D. officially moved into my Daddy Buck's room. I don't think it fooled anyone, but for appearances sake J.D. felt more comfortable since I insisted on him moving into the house with me. Sam was so happy to have him back to take charge he didn't care where he slept. I'd a sworn his grin almost cracked his face.

After a day working on getting back into the workings of the ranch J.D. came in for dinner to find me sitting at the huge partner's desk. I looked up at him as he came in and hung his hat on the peg by the front door.

"J.D.! How'd things go today?"

"I'd say pretty well. The construction crew will be laying the foundation for the barn starting tomorrow. How did the day go for you?"

I got up and came to him and put my arms around him and gave him a kiss. "Pretty well. I'll tell you all about everything after you've had a shower. Phew! Boy, you do smell."

When J.D came out with a fresh shirt I had moved to the sitting area and sat on the bull hide sofa. I had made a cool drink for him.

"Come on over here and sit with me and I'll tell you what I've been up to."

He sat down next to me and took the drink that I offered. He took a sip. "Man, that is good."

After another sip he said, "Okay, Honey, tell me what you have been doing all day while the men of the ranch have been working their asses off in the hot sun."

"Well, J.D., it looks to me like you still have a little ass to work off. But enough talk about pleasures of the flesh."

I sat back against the sofa. "I spoke with the insurance company today and they are going to bring charges against Jake."

"That sounds like a good thing."

"It is, it's just I need to go in tomorrow with John Twofeathers and tell them what we know. I would like you to go with us so you can give a description of the buckle."

"That sounds like a logical thing to do. Sure, I'll go with you. Why do you sound so hesitant?"

"Oh, I don't know. I just thought that you might not be comfortable being around John is all."

"Why wouldn't I? We owe a lot to John Twofeathers. Without him, right now you would be facing a jury for the burnin' of your own barn."

"We will be meetin' him at the agents office in the mornin' to have each of us give a statement. Then I guess it's over except to get the construction finished."

I leaned over and kissed J.D., thinking it was good that he wasn't jealous of John. I needed both of them to set this whole mess behind me.

* * *

The next morning John was waiting on a bench outside the insurance office's rustic facade on the board walk. J.D. stuck his hand out to John.

"Good mornin', John. It sure was nice of you to come to our aid like you did. If you hadn't showed up Honey sure would've been in a pickle."

"Well, J.D., I can't rightly say that it would've felt right if I hadn't. I guess it was just a good turn of luck that I had been where I was, when I was." Big John flashed me that big beautiful smile. J.D. noticed, but didn't say anything.

The agent talked with us one at a time. Our testimony was recorded. It was my guess that they interviewed each of us separately to make sure that our stories matched up. The agent came out and shook our hands.

"Miss Durbin. It was nice of you to come all this way. Especially Mr. Twofeathers and Mr. Colby. Sheriff Hobbs has told the Company that Jake Tallmadge left town and is nowhere to be found. I guess as far as he is concerned the case is closed. But I want to tell you that we don't feel that way at all; we have our investigators working on it. After all, there is a quarter of a million dollars that he is responsible for us losing. We want restitution for that. And Mr. Colby, just to let you know, we have a bulletin out to all the pawn shops about your buckle. Just in case Jake tries to pawn it."

J.D. gallantly took a hold of my elbow as we walked out toward the parking lot to where both vehicles had been parked. As he opened the door for me to get in Big Red I stopped and turned to John.

"John, would you like to join us for lunch? I'll buy."

John looked at J.D. and smiled.

"Naw, Honey. I got to get back to Chisholm's. We got lots of vaccinating to do this afternoon. Old man Chisholm let me off this morning so I could come in and testify for you. But thanks anyway." He tipped his hat to me and J.D. then climbed up into his old Bronco's cab. It started up with a rattle and wheeze, then roared to full life as all the cylinders finally caught.

I finished getting into Big Red and J.D. closed the door and went around to the driver's side.

"J.D.?"

"What?"

"Do you think they'll ever catch Jake?"

"That I don't know. But I am just as happy if they don't."

J.D. put his hands on the steering wheel and turned his head to me. "I want the Double D to get back on its feet. Because, Honey Durbin, I love you. I want all this behind us so that you can focus on us. Before all of this, we were getting married. I don't know if even that thought has entered your mind lately."

"Why, J.D., you know I love you very much. It won't be long before everything will be just fine. We can think about getting married then."

J.D. reached down and turned the key in the ignition. Big Red's engine bellowed like a bull coming out of the chute, ready to roll. J.D. gave me a last look before turning his attention to navigating out of the civic center parking lot. I don't know what else was on his mind because he never spoke about anything on the rest of the way home. I didn't mind; I had my own thoughts about what the next day would bring. The barn and equipment issue seemed to be settling itself now that the arson charge had been dropped. What weighed on my mind was money. With the shortfall it was going to be tough. A thought popped into my mind as we drove into the ranch yard.

CHAPTER TEN

J.D. came around to let me out of Red.

"Honey, you're smiling. My, you sure look pretty when you smile. I don't recollect that I've seen it too much lately."

"Well, J.D., I may have just figured us a way to make ends meet. Would you go get Sam and come back into the house for some lunch? I've got something to discuss with you both."

When Sam and J.D. arrived, I was at the desk looking over the computer screen. I hit the print button and the printer hummed out a sheet of paper.

"You two go sit at the table. Juana will be serving lunch in just a moment. I have something to discuss with you both that just might get us back on track."

The two men looked at each other with an *Oh no what has she got up her sleeve now?* look.

Juana brought out a large plate of sandwiches, a large pitcher of sweetened ice tea and a cake plate with a coconut cake sitting on it. "You two come sit down and eat lunch. I just baked this cake this morning."

I gathered the printed paper and came over to the table and sat down with the men.

"When we were leaving the insurance office..."

"Excuse me, Honey, how did that go?"

"Why, Sam, I'm sorry. It went very well. They are going to do a full up investigation on the whereabouts of Jake Tallmadge. They are pressing charges. It seems that they have the clout necessary to get the wheels turning from our law enforcement agency, namely Sheriff Hobbs. We don't have to do anything more."

"Yeah, Sam, it looks like they want him almost as bad as we do."

"Well, that would sure beat the devil around the stump if they catch him."

"Oh, they'll catch him alright. Remember, they had to fork over two hundred and fifty thousand dollars." I paused. "Now as

I was saying, when we came out of the insurance office I began thinking how we would make ends meet until the next rodeo season. And I may have come up with an idea."

J.D. and Sam leaned in closer to me.

"Maybe I could step up the sale of the frozen sperm from old Nero. We had initially decided that we wouldn't flood the market with it; only sell outside our own stock a couple a year. But we have enough to inseminate maybe a hundred cows. There might be enough in cryo to help get over the hump of bad luck."

I looked at the two men. They sat there a minute letting what I had said sink in. J.D. was the first to speak. He turned to Sam.

"You know something? I think she has a good idea."

"You durn tootin' she has a good idea. I'm surprised that I didn't think of it."

"And fellas, that's not all. I figure that we will contact the rodeo contractors and set up some deals this year for next year's rodeo season. You know, get the jump on things and give them a discount for signing early."

J.D. interjected. "The construction crew has got a good start. We are adding a couple of new features like we all talked about. Besides a combination office and tack room for the foreman, there will be a section for a medical emergency room."

"Yeah, Honey, it'll be real nice. Like your daddy wanted but just never got around to puttin' in."

"Yeah, Sam, there was a lot Daddy Buck never got around to doin' after Momma died." I let out a sigh. "But now I guess ol' Jake kinda did us a favor. In an ass backwards sort of way."

"Well, if I see him before the Sheriff gets to him, there might not be enough left to mop up a floor with."

"I agree with you there, J.D. I got a score to settle with him big time. But he ain't worth our while even worrying about right now. It'd be my guess that he is a long ways from here."

The plate of sandwiches was gone and Sam was eyeing the cake sitting on the table. It had been a long while since we could just sit and talk without some sort of catastrophe to work through.

"Why don't you go ahead and cut that cake there, Sam? I don't want you to die of dehydration from the way you're droolin' all over the place."

Sam reached over and pulled the cake plate over to him and picked up the knife. He cut three large pieces and put them out on the small plates that Juana had put out for the purpose.

I freshened up our glasses with more tea and proposed a toast. I held my glass up high.

"To the Double D and its cowboys, who come out of the chute spurrin' and don't let go 'till the buzzer sounds."

J.D. added to the toast.

"And to its cowgirl who looks pretty in pink, but is wicked with spurs."

I didn't want to mention to either Sam or J.D. the feelin' I had down deep in my gut. Didn't want to spoil the moment. It'd been a tough time for me, that's for sure, but it had been a tough time for them also. Now it looked like everything was working out. But in the back of my mind I had this feeling that we hadn't heard the last from Jake. Maybe I had gotten to be a pessimist but I couldn't shake the feelin' that there was something brewing in the wind, kinda' like when a sand storm was brewing. There is this kind of electricity in the air, where everything you touch sends off sparks, sand grit gets between your teeth and you can't get rid of it by drinking a glass of water. That kind of feelin'. No, I didn't want to spoil it for the men. They might just need a little coconut cake and a relaxed afternoon to draw to. I knew I sure did.

CHAPTER ELEVEN

The next couple of weeks the construction caused a big enough ruckus around the ranch that the stress on the pregnant cows had become evident. Some of them were off their feed a bit and acted nervous. A nervous Brahma is not good to work with. They can be real dangerous if they get scared. The heavy equipment must've looked like fire breathing, noisy and bad smelling monsters to them; they all were nervous. So we thought it best to pen them up in the pasture as far away as possible from the construction. The conditions were cramped in comparison to what the cattle had become used to. But they would survive. It was just a short while.

A short while is all it takes.

I had just come in from a meeting with Mr. Pickett, getting his advice on how to approach the contracts folks for next rodeo season. As I pulled Red up into the yard I noticed that ol' Doc Baxter's truck was in the yard. He had been the Double D veterinarian ever since I could remember. The nice thing about large animal vets is that they do house calls. But what the hell was he doin' out here?

Sam, J.D and the doc were coming out of the pasture walking real slow. From the looks on their faces it wasn't good, whatever it was. I got out of the truck and walked over to them.

"Howdy, doc. I hope you're here for a social call."

"Miss Durbin, I sure wish it were so. But Sam here called me out to look at your cows."

My eyes darted to Sam. "What's the matter, Sam?"

"Well, Honey, you know that the cows been off their feed and kinda' cranky lately. We all just made the assumption that it was because of the construction work goin' on. Didn't pay a lot of attention other than to move them out to the edge of the pasture."

"Okay, so why is the doc here?"

Doc Baxter spoke up. "Miss Durbin, the fact of the matter is that the stress and the closeness of the cramped condition in the small pasture has caused an outbreak of Bovine Rhinotracheitis in them."

I couldn't say a word for a few minutes. "What do we do? The Double D ain't never had a distemper outbreak before. We've always been successful and vigilant with vaccinations. Our stock has always been healthy."

"Miss Durbin. It is because you take such good care of your stock that I think the prognosis is good that you and the cows will come through this."

"Doc, what about the calves? Those cows are six months pregnant."

"I know that. I'm the one that signed the certificate of insemination."

"Well?"

"Survival is ninety percent. That is all I can say. It is a highly contagious, infectious disease that is caused by Bovine Herpesvirus-1. In addition to causing respiratory disease, this virus can cause conjunctivitis, abortions, encephalitis, and generalized systemic infections. It remains inactive until the animal is placed under stress. The virus causes secretions from the eye, nose and reproductive organs. Right now your cows have respiratory tract infections."

Doc took off his green John Deere baseball cap and replaced it on his sweating head.

"But I'd say we caught it at the beginning of the infection before it could spread to the others. Thanks to Sam here."

Doc reached over and patted Sam on the shoulder.

"Well now, Doc, these girls are mine to look after." Sam blushed just a little bit. Sentimentally he looked at all the Double D as his ever since Daddy Buck hired him.

We reached the doc's truck and as he stowed his black bag he spoke directly to me. "I've given all the instructions there to J.D. and Sam on what to do. If you send one of the hands in I will give them some antibiotics. The good thing is that they are already separated from the rest of the ranch cattle, so we should have a good chance that the virus won't spread."

With that said, he got into his truck and just as he put it in gear added, "Miss Durbin, I'll have the antibiotics ready by tonight."

I waved a weak goodbye to him as he drove out of the yard. Sam and J.D. came over to me.

J.D. spoke. "Honey, the doc said we have to separate all the cows into individual pens. They can't share their food or water. The virus is transferred through the mucus that is expelled from their mouth and nose."

I was still numb with the news. *Damn, I must be payin ' back for some karmic wrong, seems if it weren't for bad luck I wouldn't have no luck at all.* "Okay. Sam, make arrangements to get some portable pipe corrals out here. The first thing is to get them cows separated. We'll need extra mangers and watering troughs for each pen. J.D., you need to get the boys together and tell them what we need to do. I think the hardest part is to get them girls to stand still for their shots and any subsequent treatment that may be needed."

"You know, it might be a good idea to construct a chute system for the inoculations. It may just make it easier in the long run. Might save a few medical bills along the way."

"Sam, the cows ain't gonna get hurt by getting a shot."

"It weren't the cows I was thinkin' about."

"Very funny. Go get Toby and Billy Bob and one of the big rigs to go get the corrals and other stuff we need."

"Honey," said J.D. "I'll get some boys together and start the chute. I'm thinking that we can put the pipe corrals over next to the loafer shed. That way we can set up a place where we can store the medicine and the other stuff we might need. The doc said we may have need for a vaporizer tent if some get bad enough. The shed has a beam and the room in it."

"That's a good idea, J.D. You go attend to it. I'll drive into Doc's and get the medication."

After the first couple of days I felt like I had been rode hard and put away wet. I ached in every part of my body. There wasn't a spot on me that didn't hurt when touched. Just the mere thought of getting out of bed in the morning made me hurt in places I had never known I had.

Everything that's done with a cow is done in a larger than life manner. The extra labor that the sick cows required put me out into the actual day-to-day grind of heavy ranch work. The ranch hands had their hands full just doing the daily chores around the place. We really couldn't put on a couple more hands, so that left me to fill in. The portables had to be cleaned every day and the watering tubs had to be scrubbed. Usually the ranch hands did the mucking and when the cattle lived in a wide open pasture there was no need.

Bottom line, my daddy finally got his wish. He had always said that I had it too easy. To appreciate what I had, I had to fight for it. *Well, Daddy Buck, your little girl is fighting for it and I have the blisters on my hands to prove it.*

CHAPTER TWELVE

CRACK!

I looked up and toward where the loud ominous sound came from. It had come from the barn building site. I could see that the crane that held the main center beam had broken into two pieces right at the focal point. I threw the pitchfork out of the pen and climbed through the pipe fence and started running toward where everyone else had, to the base of the long fulcrum arm of the crane used to place the large, metal I-beam in place that would be the support for the roof of the two story barn.

The beam and the crane arm descended down onto the new walls of the barn, slicing them like a knife cuts butter.

Dust had risen up when it had fallen and as the beam settled, the dust also set enough to be able to see if anyone had gotten hurt. J.D. came to a halt at the same time and place I did.

"What the hell happened?"

"Is anyone hurt?" I shouted out as I quickly scanned the group of men that had gathered, to make sure everyone had been accounted for.

Toby came over to where I stood gaping at the large heavy metal bit of wreckage.

"Damn, Miss honey, lucky no one was working in there."

"Yeah, Toby, we are lucky."

The crane operator climbed down out of the cab of his machine and came trotting over to where I was standing looking at the wreckage.

"Miss Durbin. I don't know what happened. I'd been using the crane all morning. I've never heard of anything like this ever to happen before."

"Well, no one was hurt. I suppose that is the main thing." I didn't know if I should curse and rant and rave, or sit down and cry. But as I looked at the damage it had done, all I could think was, God almighty, look at the mess. "We'll have to clean it all up before we can even get back to rebuilding what was lost."

J.D. had climbed over to where the crane arm had separated and was looking at the cable all intermingled with the pulleys. I could see that he had seen something in the twisted mass. I yelled over to him.

"Whatcha' find?"

He didn't say, just waved his arm at me to come and see. I picked my way to where he had crouched down. He reached his hand out and pointed to a large bolt that had sheared off.

"This here bolt broke under the weight of the I-beam. But it looks like it had some help."

I could see what he pointed at. The bolt had been cut about halfway through.

"J.D., you think someone actually sabotaged the crane?"

"It shore looks like it. I think that we need to call Sheriff Hobbs and the insurance investigators."

I could feel my face begin to get hot and tears starting to form in my eyes. I didn't want the hands to see me. "J.D., get the boys back to work and tell the construction crew that they are done for the day."

How much more could I stand of this streak? I got up and turned toward the house and pushed past everyone that was standing around. Once in the house I let go with the waterworks. A torrent poured out of me. Then I dried my eyes and called the Sheriff's office. Sheriff Hobbs said he would send someone out as soon as possible.

The insurance investigator said he would be out within the hour. It never ceased to amaze me that when there is money involved, how quickly you can get help. I couldn't help but laugh a little about the insurance company and how attentive they are to what happens at the Double D when it was their money they got bilked out of. They didn't much care when it had been the Double D's.

The investigator came out and examined the broken crane. He gave me a short review of his findings. "Yep, the bolt has been cut through halfway. It would've held for a time, then let go just when enough weight had been put on it. Any ideas as to when someone coulda done it?"

"Not really. It had to have been sometime in the night. The crane has been here a couple of weeks, but it isn't used every day. There's always someone here at the ranch."

"Well, it had to be someone that wasn't afraid of heights and fit enough to shinny up the crane arm. Actually, once he got up there no one would see him. A hacksaw wouldn't make much of a sound. They'd only have to worry about the going up and the coming down."

"Do you think that we all were wrong about Jake having left town?" I looked between J.D. and the investigator.

"Well, Miss Durbin, it's my guess that he is our best suspect so far. That is, unless you've pissed someone else off real bad. Bad enough to want to maybe commit murder."

* * *

After the Sheriff's deputy came out and I had made a statement and got the evening's administrations to the cows completed, I dragged my body into the house. Juana had dinner on the table but I didn't feel much like eating. I had a lot going through my head. Sam was cow-sitting. It looked like most of the cows were going to pull through but there was one that had been really laid low. We put her into the tented pen in the loafer shed. Doc Baxter said that she might pull through but we would probably lose the calf. So Sam decided that she was his priority. Juana took him some supper.

J.D. came in and put his hat on the peg by the door. He sat down on the chair in the living room. For some reason I snapped, "It's all your fault, you know."

He turned to me with a look of *what the hell?* "My fault?"

"Yeah, your fault. Everything was going along just fine until you showed up here at the ranch."

"Hold on there! If I recall, you invited me to come on out and stay awhile."

"It was you that wheedled your way into my Daddy's good graces, with that 'I want a ranch like this someday.' crap."

"If I remember right, I brought you home that night that Nero died. You were in no shape to drive, so I brought you home."

"Yeah, you brought me home alright. You saw what a nice set up that we had here and you decided that you wanted a piece of it. You had just brought the ranch owner's only daughter home. That put you in the okay place with the rich ranch owner and you took advantage of it."

"Honey, I've pulled your fat out of the fire so many times. It's getting tiresome."

"What do you mean by that!"

"That night; at the Stompin' Grounds. You remember the night you almost got raped because you were rubbing yourself all over some guy from the city?"

"What about the real reason we are having issues with Jake right now? When you managed to get yourself made ranch foreman. That caused me to let Jake go."

"I didn't have anything to do with that and you know that."

"Well, I should of kept Jake and let you go. Then none of this would have ever happened."

"Honey, you don't believe that, do you?"

"Yes, I do."

"Honey, I thought you loved me! You asked me to come back, because you loved me and you needed me."

"Hell, yes, I needed you. The Double D needed you. Where else would I get a foreman that knew the ranch and how it worked. You were the perfect pick. And you came cheap too. Just an occasional fuck."

The look on J.D's face made me realize that I had gone too far.

He didn't say another word. He got up and went to his room and packed his bag and left. Not even a glance back at me.

When the door slammed I looked up to see the face of Juana in the kitchen doorway. She didn't say anything either. Just turned her head and went back to doing the dishes.

I stood in the middle of the floor for a long moment and then went to the front door and laid my head on it and with my fingertips traced a heart shape on it and the initials "J.D.".

CHAPTER THIRTEEN

Tired, confused and lonely, sleep just wouldn't come to me. My bed could have been full of rocks for all the comfort I got out of it. I looked at the clock. Two a.m. The bedroom window was open to let in what breeze there was. The lacy curtains fluttered, almost like they waved to me to come see. I swung my legs over the edge of the bed and looked out. There was a light on in the shed out by Nero's pasture. Funny, I didn't recollect ever really calling it that before. Sam must be up. He had almost lived out there for the last couple of weeks. Especially since Molly Bee took a turn for the worst. She was the cow that had been put in the tented pen. Doc Baxter said she'd most likely abort her baby.

Sam had named her after an old Country Music star from the Grand Ole Opry that he had liked when he was a young man. It had been hard news for him to hear from Doc; this would have been Molly's first calf.

I got dressed and careful not to wake Juana slipped out of the house and went out to the shed. Sam sat on his cot with a mug of coffee in both hands. He looked up when he heard me come around the corner. I could hear the deep rattle of Molly's breath.

"How's she doin'?"

"Better, I think. At least Doc Baxter thinks so. Looks like she'll pull through." He sighed. "It don't look so good for the calf. Doc can't hear a heartbeat."

"Oh, Sam, I'm sorry."

"It happens sometimes. There have been stillborn calves before."

"Got any more of that coffee?"

"Yeah, I just made a fresh pot, it's real strong." He looked up at me, then at his watch. "What are you doing up at this hour?"

"J.D. left."

"I know. He came and said goodbye."

I poured myself a cup of the hot liquid, took a sip and walked over to where I could see Molly through the plastic sheeting. The cow's breath came in hard panting noises.

I sat in the straw just outside her pen. "When's the last time you had a break, Sam? You look tired."

"I'm okay, Honey. Me and my old hide do quite well out here on my old cot. I look tired cause I'm old. Besides, you've had enough on your plate lately."

"You know J.D. is most likely gone for good."

"He seemed pretty hurt when he left."

"Sam, why do you suppose he came back after the first time?"

"My guess is that the boy really loves you."

"You don't think he is just after the ranch?"

Sam looked at me like I had just sprouted a horn out of my forehead. "Hell no, gal! Why would anyone in his right mind stick around here with all the stuff that's been goin' down lately? I cain't think of a man alive that would be so desperate to get a hold of a ranch with as much bad luck as we've had lately. Hell's bells, woman, the man loves you. If you can't see that then you ain't as smart as you think you are."

"He says the only thing that I love or care about is the Double D."

"Well, is he right?"

I never got the chance to answer Sam's question because right then Molly started into her labor. Her breathing was rasping and came in hard pants. The cow had already been lying down but now she was over onto her side. Her water broke and black blood gushed out. Sam and I jumped to her aid. Mercifully because of her weakened condition all she needed to give was a couple of hard pushes and the calf's head and shoulders were clear. I grabbed and pulled it the rest of the way out. Doc Baxter was right. The calf was dead.

I dragged the body out and off to the side of the barn and covered it up with an old saddle blanket so nothing would get at the carcass until a little later when I would have the boys come and get it to be buried.

Sam was cleaning Molly up and trying to console her. I couldn't help thinking that she knew. Somehow I felt that she knew that she had just lost her baby. Tears streamed down my cheeks. God never gave animals the ability to cry so I cried for her.

By the time that we got Molly all comfortable again the sun had started to rise and there were waking up sounds coming from the bunkhouse. That meant that in a couple of hours I would have to tell the men that J.D. had left and that they would be taking their orders from me directly. To be honest, I wasn't quite sure how that was gonna go over with the men. Seemed to me they knew that the orders came from me, that the delivery system just came from either Sam, or J.D., never directly.

I needed to get up to the house and get cleaned up before I gave them the news. I could smell breakfast cooking when I came in the front door. I poked my head into the kitchen. Juana was busy at the stove.

"Juana, just a light breakfast for me this mornin'. I ain't very hungry. But I'm sure Sam could use a good one. He's been busy all night. Molly lost her calf. I'm thinkin' that some ham and eggs might brighten his mood a bit."

"Honey, I am sooo sorry to hear about the calf. Is Molly gonna be okay?"

"I believe so. I got to go get cleaned up. I'll be out in a few."

* * *

I stood on the porch waiting until all the ranch hands had gathered. While I waited, my thoughts drifted back to when Daddy Buck, Sam and I had stood in this very same place to explain a change that would impact the ranch operations. I didn't have the butterflies in my stomach then like I did now.

"Men, I called you all here first to thank you all for doing so well under the circumstances. I also feel that you need some explanation about what is going on with the Double D."

I looked out among them. Some had a sheepish look on their face and stared at their boots or hands, everywhere except at me.

"Right now the Double D is solvent. That means we have more than enough resources to meet all of our obligations, so there is no need for any of you to worry about your jobs."

A murmur went around the group.

"That's alright. I knew that thought had occurred to at least a few of you. But there is no worry. The other thing that I know is worrying you is the crane accident." I paused for a moment. "The crane breaking and falling was not accident. A bolt had been sawed half through."

Toby shouted out, "Miss Honey, do we have any idea who would do such a thing?"

"We think that it most likely was the same one that burned the barn down. The authorities and myself believe that it was Jake Tallmadge in both cases."

A tall cowboy from a row back raised his hand.

"Yes, Slim."

"Miss Honey, are we 'spectin' to have any more 'accidents' round here?"

"I truly can't say. We thought that Jake had lit out and would have been out of the state by now."

The men looked at one another and then back toward me.

"I only have two more things to tell you and then it's back to work. The first is that J.D. has left the Double D, and I don't believe he will be back. The second thing is that I will assume all his responsibilities while Sam takes care of getting the recovering cows back on their feet."

I searched all of their faces to see if I could tell how they received the news. Nothing. I couldn't tell if that was good or not. All I knew was that the answer to Sam's question of which one did I love more, J. D. or the Double D, kept ringing in my ears. As I looked at the fifteen faces before me I realized that it was more than just me and my problems; it was the problem of everyone on the D.

"Okay, men, that's all I have for now. Just be careful and double check any equipment that you use to see if there's been tampering."

The men slowly walked away and went about their daily chores and duties. Most of them knew what to do without much direction. Toby was the newest and he had been here the last two years.

I felt bone weary and I needed J.D. I came to the conclusion that I loved him more than the ranch. My problem was how to prove it to him. I had hurt him bad. Real bad. Would he be willing to try a third time?

CHAPTER FOURTEEN

I couldn't sleep. Too tired was my guess. As I tossed and turned in my bed filled with rocks and the events of the last week, I heard something. My first thoughts were that Juana had come back early from a week-long visit with her family. My brain ruled that out. She would never have done that without letting me know about it first. Besides, I would've had to go get her at the bus station. No. It was not her.

The sounds were coming from the living room area of the house.

My bare feet eased to the floor as I slipped my robe on and crept over to the door tying the belt. I pulled it tight as I put my ear to the wooden panel.

It sounded like someone was hurriedly looking for something. The sound was of drawers being opened and of paper being shuffled. A curse. The slamming of the drawers onto the floor.

Whoever it was didn't seem to care if anybody heard him. *Damn, the guns were all in the gun case right where the intruder was.*

I looked around the room for a weapon.

Nothing.

My cell phone was sitting in its recharging stand. In the living room.

The sounds were getting louder. It sounded to me whoever it was had lost all care about being discovered. That thought made my skin crawl a bit.

I had to think of something. *The window?* No. I had to confront whoever it was. I decided what they were looking for had to be the cash box. The cash box that had twenty-five thousand dollars in it, the ranch's monthly payroll. I couldn't afford the loss.

Then I spied Nero's PRCA trophy sitting on the dresser. I picked it up and as quiet as I possibly could opened my bedroom door.

I crept to the archway between the hall and living room and peeked around the wall.

A beam of light searched the walls. It came from a dark figure that held the torchlight out in front washing the room in a yellowish glow. I gripped the trophy tightly and held it high in my right hand like a battle club. I reached in and flipped on the light switch.

The illuminated figure looked up in surprise as the light showed me the intruder was Jake Tallmadge.

"Jake! What in the hell do you think you're doin'?"

He looked at me as if I was a complete stranger. I could see the anger and madness in his eyes and the snarl of his upper lip.

"Where's the box?" He spat out the words. I could see spittle that had escaped his mouth as it trickled down his chin, like a rabid dog.

"What box are you talkin' about?"

"The metal box where you keep the payroll in."

My first reaction was to try and reason with him.

"Now, Jake, you don't want to do anything rash. You're already in trouble enough."

"Never you mind what I want and don't want. Where is it? I know you got it somewhere. You moved it from the desk drawer. I already checked there."

I looked over to the mess of scattered papers strewn all over the floor and the drawers that had been dumped.

"Now, Jake, what makes you think that I have that kind of money just sitting around here in the house?"

"The Durbins always kept the payroll in cash here in the house."

"Jake, there have been lots of changes here at the Double D since you left."

Jake started to take a step toward me. I raised the trophy higher and leaned my arm back so I could get a stronger swing into it.

He hesitated for just a second, then he lunged toward me.

I started my swing and his hand came up and grabbed my wrist. He used the flashlight to swing at my head and hit me with a glancing blow. It stunned me just enough that I dropped the trophy I had so desperately clutched as my only available weapon.

I went down on my knees. He came at me like a madman.

"You high and mighty bitch."

He grabbed my arm and with his flashlight as a club, swung it up and hit me again, this time more solid. I blacked out.

* * *

My eyes blinked at the brightness as I woke up. I could hear the rhythmic metallic beep, beep, beep to my left as it worked its way into an insistent and painful throbbing in my head. Daddy always told me, "If you could feel pain it meant you were still alive." It made me realize if pain was to be my measure, then I most surely was not dead. My stomach felt as if I had been kicked by a mule. I squinted against the light as I looked around. There were flowers sitting next to me on a small table. I turned and looked at the other side and there stood a metal pole with an IV bag hanging onto it with a tube that extended down to the back of my hand.

"Looks like you're back amongst us living."

That voice belonged to Sam. I had heard it all my life. I opened my eyes wider and saw the old man sitting in a chair next to the window.

I tried to speak but my throat was dry. I managed a cracked croak. "Water, please."

Sam got up and poured me a glass of water with a straw in it and held it for me to take a drink.

I swallowed it. It tasted better than the best Champagne I'd ever tasted.

"Now, Honey, you just take it easy. You had a bad go of it."

The room swayed a little bit, I closed my eyes then opened them. The room had stopped.

"What happened, Sam?"

He dragged the chair up to the bedside and took a seat.

"Well now, Honey, near as we could tell ol' Jake broke into the house and was looking for the payroll. He knew that we always paid the boys in cash. So he musta' figured that he would get his-self one."

I motioned for another drink. Sam helped me, then continued.

"Anyways I had heard all the commotion up at the house and by the time I had pulled my boots on to investigate, I heard you scream." Sam gave a chuckle. "I tell you, girl, these old legs of mine can still remember how to run when they sense trouble." He blushed a little.

"Anyways, I busted in the front door with mah gun just in time to see Jake, that son-of-bitch, hit you with his flashlight. I took a shot at him and missed 'im, damn it all."

I gave Sam a weak smile and patted his hand.

"Well," he went on, "that mangy cur split out the back door and by the time that the other boys got there he had done lit out to whatever rock he's been hidin' under."

"How long ago was that, Sam?"

"Bout three days. You had us all worried plumb to death."

I reached up and felt the bigness of the bandages around my head.

"Yah look like one of them there Ayy-rabs with that on your head. But the doc says it won't be long before you can have it taken off."

"When can I go back home?"

"The doc says you need to stay here for a couple more days, then if you take it real easy you can come on back to the ranch. Juana is getting everything taken care of at the house."

"What are you gonna do, Sam? You're down a man with me in here and looks like I won't be much help for a while."

"Well, don't you fret about that right now. You need to just get well. J.D said he would come out and help until you get back on your feet."

I couldn't help but get my hope up. "J.D. is back?"

"Naw. He said he owed Daddy Buck, so he's only come back to help while you're laid up."

"Oh Sam! I've really messed up with him, haven't I?"

"Yeah, Miss Honey, I'd say when you screw up, you do it right well."

As I turned away from Sam's vision my head throbbed and tears formed in my eyes. The old man patted my shoulder and said, "I got to go on back to the Double D. The hands all want to know how you are."

"Sam."

"Yes'm."

"When you find out, will you tell me?"

"Tell you what, Miss honey?"

"How I am. I don't know anymore."

CHAPTER FIFTEEN

The day I came home from the hospital Juana rode in with Sam to fetch me home. I still wasn't allowed to wash my hair but the large bandage had been gone for a day. There was a spot where there had been surgery that left kind of a stubbly tennis ball fringe where it had started to grow back in. I was a bit depressed about it.

"Juana, look at my hair. What can we do about that?"

"Ai, Mi'ja, you worry too much. You know I'll fix it for you."

She plunked a satchel she had brought onto the bed and dove into it.

"First we clean the hair."

I'm not sure what she used but it was waterless, and it felt so good to have my hair clean and smell of something other than antiseptic. Then she began to work on my face with some heavy-duty concealer for the bruises on my face, followed by my regular makeup. When Juana was satisfied, she held up a mirror. She had combed my hair into a side sweep. I couldn't see any of the stubble. I had to really look very hard to see the traces of any bruise along the side of my face.

"Juana, you are a gem. The boys at the ranch will think I have been vacationing."

I reached up to give her a hug. "Thank you!"

The middle-aged woman fought away tears in her eyes. It was my guess that she partially blamed herself for what had happened. "Hurry up now. We got to get you out of these horrible hospital clothes."

"Why, Juana, don't you think that the split tail down the back is a rather fetching fashion statement? I'm sure it would be all the rage with the boys."

"Ai, Honey. Shame on you." She tsked at me, grabbed my arm and helped me to stand. "I brought you a pretty pink shirt for your homecoming."

The drive on the way home was filled with Juana telling me all about the mess that she faced when she came home, and what had gotten broken. I'm not sure that the good mood I had pretended to be in at the hospital would have lasted much longer so I was very grateful for us pulling up into the D's yard.

I gave a wave and a smile to all the boys that had gathered to welcome me home. I didn't see J.D. in the group. I gingerly walked up the porch steps and when I stepped into the living room, it looked like a florist shop with floral arrangements everywhere there was a flat surface. But the impact of the flowers paled for me by the sight of J.D. sitting at the desk. He had been going over the books from the look of him. He laid the pencil down when he saw me.

"J.D. I didn't expect that you'd be in here."

"Well, where else would I be, Honey? You needed someone to manage the ranch while you were away. Who better than me?"

Right then I felt a little dizzy. "J.D., I'm glad right now to have you but we can talk later. Right now I am afraid that I need to lie down for a little while. Maybe after dinner we can talk?"

Juana didn't give him any time to answer me. She hustled me off to my bedroom. I must say it was nice to lie back in my own room. Hospitals are not the place for any rest. I must have fallen asleep for a while because it was dark when I woke up.

I came out of my room and was a little surprised to find that J.D. was still there. He was watching television and jumped a little when I spoke.

"Hello, J.D."

"Honey, I didn't hear you come in." He started to get up.

I waved him to stay seated. "I'm not making much noise these last few days." I tried to make light of the situation.

When I sat down I needed to close my eyes, getting up and sitting down made me a little dizzy.

"Honey, are you all right?"

"Yes. I'm alright. At any rate I am better off here at home than at the hospital. Besides, there is too much to get done."

"Yeah, Sam told me how you've been working."

"Well, Sam tends to exaggerate sometimes. But tell me, how did you find out what happened? I thought that you headed off to parts unknown. You know, got back on the circuit."

"I decided to hang around for a while. I rented a spot for my camper at the KOA down the road from the Stompin' Grounds. That's when a couple of the D's boys came in and were talkin' about what had happened to you."

"So, once again Honey Durbin gets bandied about at the local bar." I shrugged my shoulders.

"Naw, Honey, it wasn't anything bad. I think the boys were trying to get a lead on where Jake might be."

"That's when you came out to see what had happened?"

"Yeah, as a matter of fact it was. You see, no matter what has happened between us, Honey, fact is I still owe Daddy Buck a thing or two."

"I..."

"I'm not finished. So when I came out and talked with Sam, he told me all that had been happening with the cattle getting sick and how hard you've been working and then to have this thing happen with Jake coming in and attacking you. I... Well just say that I seen my chance to give a little pay back."

"J.D., what I wanted to tell you was that when Molly aborted her calf I realized that it was you that I loved and want."

"What! A cow aborting her calf made you realize that you really love me? Well, ain't that romantic."

"No! J.D., let me explain. Remember that night that Jasmine had her Little Nero? It was in the same place that Molly lost her baby. I took it to be a sign."

"A sign?"

"Yeah, you know, like a sign that it was time to move on with my life. Look at things a little differently."

J.D. stood up and walked around the room a bit. "Look, Honey, we tried to make a go of it twice. It didn't work out, so let's just let it go at that. And when you are back on your feet I'll be moving on."

"I know that I hurt you, but I'm sorry. It's you that I love and no one else. Nothing else."

"Honey, I'm sorry too, but I been down this road with you before. I'm not as dumb as I look. The ranch will always come first with you."

"Then quit being so dumb now. I love you."

"Then prove it!"

"I don't know how, J.D. I don't know how."

"Well then, you need to figure it out because as soon as you're able to take over the managing of this ranch again, I'm gone."

I just sat there my hands in my lap, not having the energy right then to even comment.

"Honey, I will see you in the morning. Right now I need to get to bed. I've had a long day." He started for the door.

"J.D."

He stopped. "Yes, Honey."

"Aren't you stayin' here in the house?"

"No, I'm not. I'm bunking in with Sam. Good night."

I slowly got up and went to my room and laid awake until early morning with dried tears in my eyes, trying to figure out how I would ever prove to J.D. that it was him that I truly loved.

CHAPTER SIXTEEN

When J.D. told me that there was no future for us because the ranch would always come first with me, it got me to thinking really hard. The weeks after he told me that, things at the D started to change for the better.

The cows all got better and we were lucky the only calf that we lost was Molly's baby, but Molly'd be just fine. The finished barn was better than before it had burned down. There were features that we never knew we needed until the bout with distemper. We had our own cryogenic chamber for sperm set up in the barn office and tack room. The barn had a facility put in for veterinary procedures. All the vet had to do was bring out his black bag and his potions and we could do just about anything here that would be needed. I could hardly believe how the business had started to turn around with J.D. and Sam at the helm.

J.D. refused to talk to me about anything other than the running of the ranch. The three of us, J.D., Sam and me, made a really good team. It looked as if, as bleak as it was the beginning of the year, we were going to end the year at the Double D with more than just the hope of a prosperous new year.

Halloween came and went and so did Thanksgiving. Juana and I were putting up the Christmas tree off to the side of the fireplace in the living room. I picked up the ornament that my mother had bought my daddy at the Sedona rodeo over twenty five years ago. It was a glass bucking bull with a rider on his back. It made me think of all the years Momma and Daddy spent making something of the ranch. They never fell out of love. And as much as they both had worked the Double D, and sacrificed for it, it would have never been a matter of choice for them as to which would have come first.

"Juana."

"Yes, mi'ja."

"May I ask a personal question of you?"

"You can always ask."

I placed the little bullrider on the tree.

"What happened to your husband?"

Juana stopped what she was doing and looked at me. "Why do you want to know after all these years?"

"Oh, I'm sorry, I have offended you."

"No... You have not offended me. It is just that you have never asked in all the years that I have worked for your family. That is all." She straightened up placed her hands at her back. "Let's stop for a while and I will make some hot chocolate while we take a break."

I followed her into the kitchen, and sat down at the table while she busied herself getting the cups and saucers out and onto the table. And while she made the chocolate, she began.

"Miguel and I met in the little town of Chihuahua, Mexico, when I was only fourteen and Miguel was eighteen. We fell in love and decided that we would get married as soon as my family would allow it. When I turned fifteen they finally said yes. The whole town turned out for the day."

Juana's eyes looked out in space as if she could see that day.

"We were married for a long time and found out that God had determined that I would not have any children of my own but Miguel still loved me. We decided that it would be best if we left Chihuahua and saved our money and applied for a visa to go up to the United States for work. It was easier in those days."

She poured the hot creamy chocolate into both our mugs, and then sat down at the table with me.

"I took jobs as a housekeeper and Miguel worked as a gardener. I am afraid that we were pretty much the same as so many others in our circumstances. But I went to school to learn English and at night when I didn't have classes I taught Miguel what I had learned. We were very happy. Then one evening Miguel was coming home in a rain storm and lost control of his car and was killed."

Juana dabbed at her eyes.

"You, my little mi'ja, were very small and I had started to work for your mother and father . They helped me to become an American citizen. When your mother died in the auto accident it reminded me so much of how I lost my Miguel that I vowed that I would take care of Señor Buck and you. I have been here ever since. The Durbin family is my family."

"What about the family you go to visit every once in a while? Don't you miss being with them?"

"Oh sí, I miss them. Those are my blood relatives. But, you. You are my chosen family. It is not easy to choose between the things you love. Sometimes it must be done. I made the choice to go where my heart is to remain. And it is here, with you."

I sat there and thought about what she had said, and snapped out of it when she poked my shoulder.

"Come on, now we must finish the tree. The Señors Colby and Sam will be here soon. Tonight is a celebration, remember. We are celebrating the return of your health tonight."

* * *

J.D. pulled his pickup in front of the house, then stomped his feet on the mat outside the door to remove some of the dirt before he came in. He placed his hat and jacket onto the peg next to the door just like he had gotten in the habit of doing. I watched and marveled at how natural an act it seemed to be. I realized how much I missed that simple gesture and since he had left the house, how empty those pegs seemed.

Sam had already been there for a while and held up his cup of eggnog in his hand, in a welcome to the party salute.

"Hey, J.D., about time you showed up."

J.D. had a sheepish look on his face as he came over to where I held out a cup of eggnog for him. He took it and sipped it right away. With the back of his hand he wiped the creamy residue off his lips.

"Well, I had some last minute things to pack up. I made arrangements to live down at the KOA campground. They gave me a good off-season deal."

I spoke up. "You know you don't need to leave the Double D. She needs you."

J.D. shot me a glance that made my cheeks glow red. In an instant I knew I had said the wrong thing. Again.

Juana came out. "Dinner is on the table and getting cold so we had all better come and get it."

We all sat down at the table while Juana asked Sam to be the host for the evening and requested that he give a toast. He stood up, held his eggnog high and spoke.

"Here is to Miss Honey Durbin, may she always look pretty in pink and keep her spurs on straight."

I wasn't sure that I really knew what he meant by that. It was so close to the toast that I had given in what seemed like an age ago. But I drank to it.

The rest of the dinner went well, with small talk about what the plans were to be for the D, and what a prosperous year we were looking forward to having, thanks to J.D. coming in to bail us out of a tough spot when he did. All too soon the evening was over and Sam went off to bed and Juana cleared the table. J.D. said that he needed to get going, there was a curfew at the KOA and he needed to get in before the gates closed. I walked him to the door.

He put his hand on the doorknob. I covered it with mine and looked up into his marvelous brown eyes. I looked for any telltale sign.

"You know you don't have to leave. I do love you."

"Honey, you know what I told you. I don't trust what you say. You have to prove to me that you love me. I don't know what that will take. I am willing to wait a while. But as long as I am here, that decision will not be made. You know where to find me."

He opened the door and stepped out into the night, leaving me there. My heart felt like I had been gored and as if it would crack right down the middle as I closed the door and thought about what Sam had said about keeping my spurs on straight.

My daddy had always told me there most definitely was a right and a wrong way to wear and use your spurs. First off, you needed to get them on straight and snugged down so they won't come loose during the ride. Then use them sparingly to get your point across or to get extra points. If you used them without thought it would throw your rhythm off and result in a low score often enough get you thrown aside with a horn in your gut.

CHAPTER SEVENTEEN

I sat on my bed going through my jewelry box deciding what to wear. It was Christmas Eve and it was the very first one without Daddy Buck. Just Sam, Juana and me. We had invited J.D. but he said he wasn't sure he could make it.

My fingers came into contact with the leather bracelet that J.D had given me last Christmas. He had made it himself. I took it out of the box and read what he had embossed on the leather. *Honey, the heart of the Double D.* I put it on and held my wrist across my heart and closed my eyes.

"Oh, Daddy Buck, if you can hear your little girl please help me to make J.D. know that I truly love him. How can the two things I love the most in the world cause me such grief? Am I wrong for wanting them both?"

I went to my wardrobe and took out a long, pink, prairie dress and put it on. *I'll bet Sam and Juana will be surprised to see me in a dress.* I brushed my hair so that it fell all around my shoulders and put just a touch of 'Pretty In Pink' lipstick on. I topped it all off with a black velvet ribbon that had an old fashioned cameo from Italy hanging from it. The cameo was my grandmother's that Momma had given me on my sixteenth birthday. When I stood before the mirror for one last look I barely recognized myself. I had always dressed in boots and jeans, trying to be the boy that I had always thought that Daddy Buck had never got. But as I stood staring at the pretty blond woman that stared back at me, I saw my mother. I saw what I truly wanted and I knew what it was that I had to do.

* * *

"Ai, Mi'ja! You are muy bonita. Turn around, let me look at you." Juana came over and took her hands and spun me around so she could see all sides of me.

"Aw, Juana, it's only a dress."

"But I didn't know you even owned a dress, and one so pretty."

I felt a bit self-conscious and wondered what kind of reaction I would get out of Sam if I got this kind out of Juana. For that matter, I wondered what J.D.'s reaction would be if he showed up. I picked up the punch bowl and carried it into the living room and sat it down on a table near the tree. I had gotten J.D. a gift just in case he did show. It was a new hat band. It was made out of woven horse hair with a silver concho in the center to hold it together.

I had just finished setting the table when I heard footsteps coming up the front porch. I went to the door hoping it was J.D. but remembered that I hadn't heard the old pickup come in the yard.

I opened the door and stood back a ways from it to allow Sam to come in. His eyes went wider than a deer hit with headlights on a dark night. "Juana! Who is this here filly? And where is Honey?"

"Come on in, Sam." I took his hat and his coat and hung them up on the pegs by the door. The old man couldn't take his eyes off me.

"What's the matter, Sam? Ain't you never seen no woman in a dress before?"

"Well, pardon me, Miss Honey, but it's just that I cain't remember ever seeing you in one before."

"Come on in and sit awhile, Juana isn't ready to set supper out yet. Get yourself some eggnog." I whispered, "You can have some of Daddy Buck's favorite brandy iffen you want."

"Don't mind if I do. It just might please him to know how much we all miss him."

"In that case, Sam, I think I'll have one with you."

I poured us both a snifter and joined Sam in front of the fireplace. It was hard not to notice that he kept lookin' at me.

"Sam, you ain't taken your eyes off me since you got here. What's the matter, did I leave something undone?"

"I'm sorry, Honey, it is just that with that dress on and the way your hair is, I cain't get over how much you look like your momma when she was about your age."

"Sam, you've been with the D a long time, haven't you?"

"Since before you was born." Sam chuckled. "I remember the night that you were born. I had seen your daddy face down the toughest bulls that they made and even tougher men. But the night that you were born he was as nervous as a long-tailed cat in a room full of rockin' chairs."

I had a lot of stories from the old man but never this one. I leaned in close so I could hear every word.

"Yes sirree Bob. I tell you, when you hit this world you came out a squallin' like you was mad at the world. And when the doc handed you to your daddy Buck, there wasn't a man ever prouder than he was at that moment. That's when he gave you your name."

"Honey?"

"Yep. He said that you were the sweetest thing he had ever seen. Even sweeter than honey."

Sam lifted his snifter, and I could see tears in his eyes. "Here's to you, Buck."

I joined him. "To you, Daddy Buck. We all miss you, Merry Christmas."

A knock at the door broke us out of our reverie.

"I'll get it, Miss Honey." Juana called out as she deposited some plates on the table and headed for the door.

My heart skipped a beat, J.D. had come after all. I felt so nervous that I thought about what Sam had said about the cats and rockin' chairs. My insides jumped about as if I had eaten a whole plate of Mexican Jumping Beans.

He came in with his hands full of presents and made an attempt at hugging Juana turning first left then right trying his best to fit her in between the packages, but only managed to tell her Merry Christmas. He made his way over to the Christmas tree with a "Merry Christmas" to Sam. He put the presents under the tree and turned toward me and I stood up to greet him.

"Merry Christmas to you, J.D. I'm so glad you could make it."

His eyes swept over me from the floor up to the top of my head and down again where they stopped at my wrist. He had seen it. The bracelet that he had made and given me last year. He didn't need to say a word, I could read it in those dark and beautiful brown eyes of his. *I had a chance. He still loved me.*

Juana came over to take his hat and coat.

"Would you like some eggnog or brandy?" I said. "Sam and I were just toasting to Daddy Buck."

"I'll have just a little eggnog. My, you sure are pretty tonight. I, ahhh... don't mean that you aren't always pretty but you look different."

"Why, thank you, J.D. I'll take that as a compliment."

The rest of the evening was spent with a lot of quiet small talk. At some time it had become a little awkward with Daddy Buck gone. It reminded me of the first Christmas after momma died. Everyone had something on their mind but no one wanted to bring it up. Me, I had made the biggest decision I had ever made in my life, and right then and there I could not tell anyone.

Ole Copper the copper horse mantle clock struck eleven. Sam yawned and announced that he needed his beauty rest. And J.D. said he had to get on back to the KOA. Both men headed out the door and I didn't do anything except show them out. "Good night to you both. Don't get run over by no reindeer."

When I turned around Juana had started to clean up the dining room. "Juana, why don't you go on to bed? It's late. Everything can wait until the morning."

She yawned. "I am a little tired." She looked around. "The food's put up. I guess the rest will wait for in the morning. Good night, Mi'ja, and Merry Christmas. May the Christ child bless you."

What I had to tell Sam and Juana could wait until morning. Or maybe the day after. I needed some time to tell them what I had decided to do. Christmas Eve and Christmas morning would not be the right time.

CHAPTER EIGHTEEN

The Stompin' Grounds hosted a big New Year Eve party and all the boys of the Double D went, except for Sam. He said he was too old and Juana didn't have anyone she said that she wanted to bring in the New Year with other than me. Me, I didn't have anyone I wanted to bring in the New Year with except J.D., and heaven only knew where he had been the last week. He hadn't returned my phone calls.

So there we sat, just the three of us.

I poured a glass of champagne for each of us and sat down. The fireplace had logs blazing. The crackling of the burning logs and the smell of the cottonwood felt homey. I took a sip to give me courage. "Juana. Sam. I've got something to tell you both and I want you to listen to me before you make any comments. Do I have your promise that you will hear me out before you say anything?"

They both gave me a look that I hope I will never see on another human being. Then each nodded their head.

Juana started to say something. I raised my finger. She stopped.

"First of all I want the both of you to know that you are my family now. I love you both and I always want you with me. But I have made a decision that is the hardest thing I have ever done in my life." I took a deep breath. "I have put the ranch up for sale."

Shock registered on Sam's face but he didn't say anything and neither did Juana. "Sam, my plans are to make a move to a small place, take a couple of the horses and Nero Junior. I'd like it if you'd come with me." I turned to look directly at Juana. "I'd like you to stay with me too. I don't know where I'll be going yet, or when I suppose it'll sell."

I waited a moment to let what I said sink in. "Sam, if you don't want to leave the D, I'll understand. You and the boys will have some time after the sale. Part of the terms of the contract require the new owners to employ all the current hands for at least a year to give them time to find a new job if they don't get along with the new owners."

Juana reached over and took my hand and squeezed it. "Of course I will stay with you. Wherever you go."

I patted her hand with mine. "Thank you, Juana. I was hoping that you didn't want to leave me. I wouldn't know what to do without you."

"Well, the boys'll sure be surprised. I guess I need to go with you too. Someone needs to take care of you and Juana."

"Sam, I don't want you to tell the boys for a little while. J.D. still hangs out with them at the Stompin' Grounds and I don't want him to know until after the sale has been made. It may take a while and... let's just say I don't want him to know right now."

Sam sat back and drained his glass and set it down. "Whew, Miss Honey, are you sure you want to do this? I mean we just got everything all straightened out financially and with the new contracts and a state-of-the-art barn."

"Yeah, Sam, I'm sure. As much as I love the Double D, and as certain that we are back on the road to full recovery, I am sure that this is what I want to do. This is the only way that I can prove to J.D. that I want him more than the ranch." I sighed. "I'm gamblin' my whole life and my momma and daddy's dreams on this decision. I'm gamblin' that he loves me."

Sam looked at me. "Well, child, I hope that it works out for us. Remember, I got a whole lifetime of hard work in this here ranch too. This has been my home for longer than you are old. But you're my only family and I love you like a daughter and Daddy Buck would never forgive me iffen I left you to your own devices. I'm willing to take the gamble on you. Besides, it's time for me retire anyway."

With that said, Sam rose up from the couch. I noticed that the old man seemed to move more slowly than before. "Right now I think I'm goin' to bed. I got a lot to think about." He turned as he went out the door. "Juana, a good night and happy New Year." I heard his boots as he stepped down off the porch, and the crunch of gravel with the first few steps toward his little house.

Juana cleared the glasses and I followed her to the kitchen. "Juana, you haven't said much."

"There is not much to say. I will go with you wherever you go. As long as you want me. That is that."

I flung my arms around her neck and hugged her tight. "Oh, Juana, it has to work. J.D. has to accept that I love him, he just has to."

I could feel her hands as she patted my head.

"I'm sure he will, my little one. I'm sure he will. Your daddy wouldn't let him get away with not."

CHAPTER NINETEEN

It wasn't a week after I put the Double D up for sale that the realtor came by and told me that we had an offer for the ranch. I guess I hadn't been expectin' to have to make a decision so fast.

"Ah...Miss Durbin. Did you hear what I said? You got your askin' price right off."

I raised my hand as if I wanted to wave off the offending words. "I heard you, Mister Channing. I guess it's just sudden-like to me. Who is the prospective buyer?"

"Funny thing, he don't want me to tell you. I had to sign a paper saying that if I did, the deal would be off. But I can tell you that he wants to keep the ranch intact and build on it."

"Well, if he wants to buy it he has to do that. Remember, Mr. Channing, that is part of the deal for the sale. The Double D ranch and business needs to stay intact." I looked Mr. Channing straight in the eye. "I mean it! It stays intact or no deal."

"Yes, Miss Durbin, that is understood by all parties. That includes all the livestock. With the exception of the cryogenic sperm bank and one Brahma yearling bull and privately owned horses. Is that right?"

I nodded my head, swallowed hard and blinked my eyes to hold back any tears that were starting to form.

"Where do we need to go to sign the papers? I want to get this over as soon as possible before I back out."

"How about you give me till tomorrow morning to get all the paperwork in order, say around five-thirty at the office."

"Okay, I'll be there."

I could tell Mr. Channing was very happy. This was most likely one of the easiest sales he had in a long, long while. Hell, his six percent would be a whole year's salary for some men. He got into his car and a small dust cloud rose up behind him just as Sam came on over. He had been watching from the new barn's door.

"Honey, was that the Realtor fella?"

"Yeah, that's him, Sam. We had an offer."

"How much?"

"Full askin' price. I go in to sign the papers tomorrow."

I turned and grabbed Sam around the neck and started to sob on his shoulder.

He patted my back.

"Oh, Sam, it's gone. It's gone. All Momma and Daddy's dreams gone."

I don't know how long we stood there in the outside barnyard. Me a-crying on his shoulder and him just letting me.

I straightened up. "Sam, you want to tell the boys that the ranch has sold and that they will be safe for at least a year?" I sighed. "I know it's a coward's way but right now I cain't look them in the eyes."

"That's okay. I am sure they will understand." He pushed me back a little ways. "You go on in the house and tell Juana the news. I'm sure she'll be anxious to know how long she has to get the household all together for the move."

*** * ***

I walked into the real estate office like a woman going up the gallows to be hanged. I felt cold all over even in my fleece jacket. The sweat trickled down my back and into the crack of my ass. My palms were all sweaty when Mr. Channing reached out to take my hand and guide me into a little cubicle. There were three chairs and a desk with a computer and printer sitting on it. A stack of paper sat next to the computer with a couple of pens laid alongside a sheaf of papers.

"Have a seat, Miss Durbin. I'll have you out of here in two shakes of a lamb's tail."

I sat there staring at the papers, not seeing them as he shoved one after another in front of me. I signed each one of them. His smile was starting to get on my nerves. His mouth moved as he explained what I signed. I didn't hear him. *How dare he be so happy when I was signing my whole life's memories away. My momma and daddy's dreams. My lifelong passion. All in the hope that the one man I loved would take me back and help me start a new life and dare to start new dreams.*

81

It was over. Just like that. The money would be transferred into my bank account within five days. There was a ninety-day escrow so I had three months to try and patch my life back together.

My legs had somehow turned to wood while I sat in that office. I went to Big Red and managed to get in the driver's seat. I don't remember the drive much but I stopped at the Stompin' Grounds when I saw J.D.'s old pickup and camper in the parking lot.

I turned the engine off and just sat in the cab for a minute trying to get the courage up to go in and confront the man I loved more than anything. "Well, girl, it's now or never."

The door of the truck seemed heavy as I opened it and slid to the graveled parking lot surface. It took my eyes a few minutes to adjust to the dim interior of the bar. There weren't very many people in at this time of day, still early. When my eyes adjusted to the twilight of the neon bar signs, I saw that J.D. sat at the end of the bar sipping on a Pearl.

I slowly walked on over to where he sat and eased myself up on the barstool next to him. He looked over at me.

"Hello, Honey. What brings you here?"

I motioned to the bartender to get me a draft. It came and I took a long drink.

"I came to tell you I was sorry."

"That all. I knew that."

"I want you to know that I love you very much."

"I know that too."

"Damn it, J.D. I sold the ranch! Lock, stock and barrel!"

He finally looked up at me.

"Now, why would you go and do a fool thing like that?"

CHAPTER TWENTY

"I did it because I love you and I couldn't figure any other way to tell you I loved you more than the Double D. That's why."

"You mean to say that you gave up all that just to prove that you love me?"

"Yes, I did. All except Nero Junior, Juana and Sam. they're coming with me. I only got ninety days to find a new place and move..."

J.D. reached over and took my face into his hands and kissed me ever so sweetly.

"Honey, will you marry me? Right now?"

"Right now?"

"Yes, right now. We can go to the Justice of the Peace and get married right now this afternoon."

I didn't know what to say.

"Yes J.D. I need to call Juana and Sam. They'll want to be there."

"You can call them on the way. I don't want nothin' to happen twixt here and the JP."

J.D. started to dig into his jeans pocket to pay the bartender.

The bartender waved his money away. "Consider it a wedding present."

J.D. and I started out the door and I started for Big Red. J.D. grabbed my hand and pulled me towards his old truck. I pulled back only a second. He looked at me and frowned. I shrugged and got in the old Chevy pickup. We got to the City Hall with only an hour to spare. Juana and Sam waited. Juana had brought me a bouquet of flowers from the house garden.

The whole ceremony took all of about fifteen minutes and I walked out of there as Mrs. Colby. We headed back toward the Double D after we picked up Big Red.

When we got in, Juana brought out one of her coconut cakes and we had cake and Champagne.

Sam said his last goodnight for the evening and retired to his little house, and Juana picked up the dishes and stacked them in the sink. "I will do the dishes in the morning. I am tired, I am going to bed early tonight."

"Good night, Juana."

J.D. and I sat on the couch in front of the fireplace with the glowing embers. Neither said a word for the longest of whiles. As I leaned up against him, I stared into the fire thinking of the day's happenings and how I would miss this house and the ranch. No more hectic life of running the Double D would leave a big hole in my heart. I counted on J.D. being able to fill it. I snuggled into him.

"Honey, let's go to bed."

I rose up and stood next to the couch and watched while he banked the fire in the fireplace and pulled the screen closed. He closed his hand around mine and led me to my bedroom.

With the door closing behind us it occurred to me that this was real. I was Mrs. Colby.

He came to me and helped me with my shirt, slipping it down off my shoulders. Nothing hurried. We had plenty of time. He kissed my shoulders and my neck, working his way down along my belly. His fingers unbuckled my belt and unzipped the jeans fly and pushed them down over my hips.

As I stood naked in front of him he looked me over as if he had never seen me before.

"Whatcha' lookin' at, J.D.?"

"Just at how beautiful you are. I'm trying to come to the understanding that you are my wife."

He hurried and shucked his clothes off as fast as he took mine off slow. We came together in the middle of the room and embraced, not just an embrace with the arms but an embrace of the whole body. We clung together so tightly that it seemed that with the heat we generated, we had melted together.

J.D. picked me up and carried me to my bed and laid me on it. He stroked my cheek with the back of his hand.

"So soft and silky, like a newborn calf's hide."

He kissed my lips deeply and enfolded me into his arms. I could feel his hardness against my belly; it told me that his want and need of me was great. He shifted his position as I opened wide for him. When he drove into me it felt like at last I was completed. I never realized that loving could be this way.

We both came a little sooner than expected but the marvelous thing was that it was together. He had matched me stroke for stroke.

I snuggled into him with my back up against him, his arms around me. It felt so very good. At that moment I would have traded all the ranches in the world for this man that held me in his arms.

"J.D."

There was no answer.

"J.D.?"

A purring sound came from him. He had already fallen asleep.

* * *

J.D. got out of bed earlier than I did. And when I went out for breakfast he had already eaten and left.

"Juana, did J.D. say where he was going?"

"No. He just said that he had to take care of some business in town and would be back in time for lunch."

A knock on the door interrupted me. Juana handed me a cup of coffee. "You go get the door. It's most likely Sam. I'll get you your breakfast."

Sam looked very happy. I let him in.

"What's fer breakfast?"

Juana called over. "Same as yesterday. Ham and eggs with hash browns."

"What are you so happy about?"

"Oh, nothing. I just think it is high time around here that a little bit of sunshine should come into our life. Don't you? I mean, look at you." His hands gestured toward me. "A new bride and all."

"A new bride whose groom seems to have urgent business elsewhere this morning."

"Honey, he'll be back soon enough. Gives us time to talk a bit. How'd it go at the real estate office yesterday? We never got to find out with you up and gettin' hitched."

"We have ninety days to find a new place and get moved."

"That don't seem too bad. Who bought the place?"

"That is what was funny about the deal. The buyer didn't want it to be disclosed to me who they were. Until after the deal went through. The only assurance that they gave me was that the new owners will abide by all the conditions that I laid out in the deal. How are the boys taking the whole thing?"

"Seems as if they are okay with it, exceptin' Toby and Billy Bob. They seem to be kinda upset about the whole thing. You know they look at you as family. Kind of a big sis."

I laughed at that. "Well, if we get a place big enough maybe they can come with us."

* * *

I decided to go for a ride while I waited for J.D. to come home so I went out and saddled up Sparky and set out across the pasture and down along the creek bed that ran along the northern end of the far pasture. The air was still crisp but the telltale signs of spring were everywhere. The trees were budding up and the water in the creek was cold and pure. The cattle in the pasture had tender green grass to nibble on. On my way back to the house I stopped off at Nero's walnut tree. I dismounted and took Sparky's bridle off and hung it over the saddle horn to let him graze. I sat down under the tree and leaned up against it. Nero Junior ambled over to me and lowered his head. Though just a yearling, he already was about fifteen hundred pounds. He looked just like his daddy.

I put my hand out to him. He lowered his big beautiful head down for me to scratch between his horns.

"You big baby."

He pushed my hand around. I wasn't scratching hard enough.

"Okay, okay." I put more effort into the scratching, then pushed him away.

"Go away, you big lug." He stood there looking at me with those soft brown eyes. I remembered about the good times. How hard I had worked to keep this ranch.

My reverie was broken by the rattling sound of J.D.'s pickup as it came to a dusty halt in the barnyard. I got up from the tree and headed in, Sparky trailing behind.

J.D. spotted me and waited for me by the pasture gate.

"Where you been, there, J.D.?"

"I had some business in town to take care of. Come on up to the house and I'll tell you about it."

Toby came over and took Sparky. "Toby, give him a good rub down for me please."

"Sure will, Miss Honey."

J.D. put his arm around my shoulder as we walked to the house.

"Now what is this all about, J.D. Colby?"

"You'll see."

Juana had a pitcher of lemonade and ham sandwiches waiting for us, but I wouldn't let J.D. sit down to eat.

"Tell me what your big secret is."

J.D. reached into his jacket pocket and pulled out a thick envelope and handed it to me.

"What's this?"

"Open it and find out."

I tore open the envelope and pulled out the documents that were inside. I unfolded them and read.

"J.D., you son-of-bitch!"

"That is not a nice thing to call your new husband."

I yelled at him. "Why did you put me through all that misery? You are a low life!"

Juana came running out of the kitchen. "What's the matter?"

"J.D. bought the Double D," I stammered. "That's what!"

"Honey, let me explain. I bought it for a wedding present."

"A wedding present? You were awfully sure of yourself. That I would want to marry you."

"Well, sure. When I saw that the ranch was up for sale I knew you loved me. I had saved up my winnings so I made an offer and put a rather large down-payment on it."

"But J.D., that don't make any sense. You could've had it and me all free and clear. Now you have a big fat mortgage."

"I know that. But now it's mine and yours. We can start out like your momma and daddy. Build something of our own. Only better, we have a head start."

"J.D. You are one hard man to understand."

J.D. reached out and swept me into his arms. "Come here, woman."

I tried to get away from him, but not very hard. His lips came down hard on mine. My arms wrapped up and around his neck and I kissed him back. I stared up into my husband's eyes, lost in the deep soft brownness in them.

The door of the living room swung open and there stood Nero Junior, all fifteen hundred pounds of him. His head filled the door. I must have left the pasture gate open and he followed me to the house.

I went to him, scolding as I approached.

"You bad, bad boy. What am I going to do with you?"

I looked over at J.D.. "What am I to do with you both?"

The answer I got was from Nero Junior. "Brwaaaaaah."

MEET SUGAR LEE RYDER

Sugar Lee was born to a pair of Wild West rodeo show performers who later became regulars with a traveling circus. It made for an interesting time growing up, to put it mildly. At three years old she was on stage having bits of paper the size of cigarettes snapped out of her fingers by her mother's sixteen foot leather bullwhip.

Since someone decided it would be useful for her to know how to read and write, she ended up at Catholic boarding school. It was an equitable trade – the nuns gave her literacy, and she gave them heartburn with her rebellious ways.

During the summer months she traveled with the circuses and rodeos, performing at the various shows with her parents. During the years with the circus she became known as 'Sno Cone Annie', and was lucky to count all kinds of special people as her friends, including Gorilla Girl, Caterpillar Man, Alligator Boy, Pin Head and many other denizens from the carnival boardwalk.

If you liked this book and wish to read other
short stories and novels by Sugar Lee Ryder,
please check out the latest at
www.sugarleeryder.com.

Enter the World of Authors
Sugar Lee Ryder & J.D. Cutler

Sagebrush and Lace

Six guns, whips and wild, wild women!

1876: Time to throw away the corsets
and draw down on the Old West.

When Horace Greeley said "Go West Young Man"
he never would have thought that two young women
would take his advice to heart. Striking out against all
odds and risking everything to be together.

Society calls them Sapphists.
Chief Sitting Bull calls them 'Big Magic'.
Buffalo Bill Cody and Wild Bill Hickok
call them friends.
Pinkerton's detectives want them alive.
Clarke Quantrill's gang of outlaws want them dead.

Two runaway women in a man's world
risk their very lives to be together.

The pages that follow provide a glimpse into
the world of *Sagebrush and Lace*.

Print and eBook Editions available
at all major eBook retailers.

SAGEBRUSH AND LACE:

SUGAR LEE RYDER
&
J.D. CUTLER

CHAPTER 1

Samantha burst through the kitchen door, running like the devil himself pursued her, claws grasping at the tail of her shirt. She rounded the corner of the marble counter, almost knocking over the cook. As it was, Samantha startled the woman into splashing hot chestnut soup onto her apron from the large copper pot in her hands.

"Mercy sakes alive, child!" the cook exclaimed.

Not stopping for apologies, Samantha bounded up the servants' staircase to her room. The delicate glass mantle of the house's gas lamp at the top of the steep passage rattled as she took the steps two at a time.

Samantha opened the door to her room. Flecks of caked mud dribbled from her riding boots and onto the polished wooden floor. She slid to a halt.

Her father, McKinley Williams, stood before her.

His arms, sheathed in the fine woolen sleeves of a burgundy frock coat, were firmly crossed. His wide, jowly face held a scowl as dark and ominous as a thundercloud. One foot, clad in an elegant English leather shoe draped in a white cloth spat, tapped out an impatient beat.

"Young lady," he growled, "you have gone against my wishes for the last time."

"Father," Samantha replied, "Let me explain—"

"Unfortunately, there is no time right now to discuss suitable punishment for you," McKinley continued. If he heard his daughter speak, he gave no sign. "Percy Hanover is waiting downstairs for you. You will immediately wash the stink of the stable off yourself and put on something suitable to receive your guest."

Samantha's father shoved past her brusquely. He jutted his chin out, gripped his coat lapels in his hands, and puffed his chest out like a purple-tinted strutting rooster. His time-honored way of signifying that he'd rendered a final judgment on a matter. He made one last comment to her in passing.

"Do try not to embarrass me or our family."

It took all of Samantha's self-control to gently close the door after he left, when every fiber of her being screamed to slam it shut. She hurried over to the side of her four-poster canopy bed. She hopped on one leg, then the other, as she tugged off her dirty riding boots and kicked them out-of-sight, out-of-mind under the bed.

Samantha followed this up by stripping off her shirt, pants, and undergarments. Barefoot, she approached the porcelain washbasin opposite the bed and snatched up the rough washcloth that hung from a brass rail at the side. Thankfully, the water remained lukewarm from when the maid had poured it earlier. Between the wet cloth and a few squeezes of lavender scent from her atomizer, she washed away the scents of leather, steed, and straw.

She squinted at her face in the mirror for a moment, making sure she'd removed all trace of dust and mud. Delicately painted bluebells danced around the carved wooden frame of the mirror, framing her long dark hair and making her expression look more cheery than she felt.

It took her a minute to select a pair of shoes that matched a cheerful, sunny-day organza frock. She slipped it over her head and reached around to lace it up the back. Stopping just long enough to run a brush through her hair and loosely pin it up, she hurried out to the top of the landing.

She forced herself to take a deep breath before going to meet her suitor, a man hand-picked by her father. A man the same age as her father. Someone who came with the impeccable quality (in her father's eyes) of 'old money'. Percy Hanover had come to look her over. To see if she would be a suitable wife.

Samantha gritted her teeth.

I'm to be paraded in front of him. Just like a prize brood mare! I'll be damned if I'm going to marry Percy Hanover. Or any man, for that matter.

But for now she had to go downstairs and pretend to be an obedient and proper young woman.

For now.

Samantha descended the staircase and entered the parlor, careful to present herself as a virtuous young woman. The demure tilt of her head and the loose gathers of her raven-colored locks softened her features.

Her father stood imposingly by the mantle, a pear-shaped snifter of brandy held firmly in one grasping hand. But her eyes came to rest on the man who sat in the wingback chair nearby. His fine, tailored clothes and impeccably trimmed vest couldn't disguise the roll of fat that bulged above his belt line. Samantha noted that his pale complexion held the damp sheen of fresh wallpaper paste, stippled with comma-shaped pock marks.

Percy Hanover, the man of her father's dreams, simply stared. His eyes all but drank in the vision of loveliness before him.

"Percy, this is my daughter," McKinley said grandly, his outstretched hand beckoning her to come closer. He gestured with the other hand. "Samantha, this is Percy Hanover, from the Lake Forest branch of the Hanovers."

Percy stood, joints creaking, and extended a pudgy pink palm.

"Eminently pleased to meet you, my dear Samantha, eminently pleased."

Samantha took his hand in hers, repressing a shudder at the clammy feel of the man's skin. He bent forward to bestow a moist kiss on her knuckles, one that reeked of burnt tobacco and her father's favorite brandy.

She noticed her father's grim look out of the corner of her eye, and then remembered to add a little curtsy to her greeting. At the last second, she added an eyelash-fluttered glance at the floor. With any luck, that gesture would appease her father.

"The pleasure is all mine, Mister Hanover."

"Oh my dear," he gushed, "do call me Percy."

Before Samantha could tackle the task of speaking her suitor's name, the maid stepped into the parlor and announced that dinner had been set out. For the next hour, Samantha could only pick at the slabs of roast lamb, ovoid mountains of boiled red potatoes, and what chestnut soup that had been saved by the cook.

Percy and her father jawboned endlessly about the sorry state of the stock market. How President Ulysses S. Grant was ruining the nation. How the newfangled game of 'baseball' would soon prove to be a silly, forgotten fad of a sport. And all the while, Samantha could feel Percy's eyes crawl over her, like a pair of mud-colored spiders.

By the time the cook brought out silver platters of scones and snifters of warmed brandy, Samantha's patience had reached its limit. She stood, her cheeks feeling flushed and warm, and then spoke her mind.

CHAPTER 2

"Father," Samantha said apologetically, "I'm afraid that I can't stay here. All of this…excitement…has gone to my head. I simply must leave."

"Certainly, girl, certainly," her father said. "Percy's seen enough of the quality of your company, I take it?"

"Oh, I dare say," Percy Hanover said. "You go rest, my darling. Your father and I have men's matters to discuss."

She said her polite goodbye to Percy, thinking that maybe her *father* should marry him. After all, they seemed to get along like a house on fire. She suppressed a giggle at the notion of the two men in the marriage bed together.

The thought threatened to send her into hysterics, so she hurried up to her room as fast as she could. Once there, she leaned against the door, busting out in laughter at the vision of the two fat old men rutting at each other.

Sometimes, the dislike that Samantha felt for her father made her chest twinge with stabs of guilt. Her mother, gone these long years, would have chided her, encouraged her to think better of the man. But she couldn't get past her father's insatiable hunger for status in Chicago's Social Register.

McKinley's churning textile mills, founded on the city's south side, had made her father rich. But those mills couldn't make her father respectable. Free of the taint of 'new money'.

Only Samantha's maidenhead could do that.

She sat down at her desk, pulled out ink, pen and paper from the drawer, and set to writing.

My Dearest Charlotte,

The time is now. We must leave as soon as you are able to make arrangements. I can be ready in two days. I need you to come to the house to visit me tomorrow so we can make our plans.

Father has caught me riding again and I fear that I may be unable to leave save for the last and final time. Then, my love, we will be together and no one can keep us apart.

Yours forever,

Samantha

Heart pounding, Samantha folded up her note, slipped it into an envelope, and pressed it closed with a hot glob of fragrant sealing wax. She rang for the maid, and then took her by the arm as she handed over the envelope as if it contained priceless jewels.

"Daisy," Samantha said, "I need you to take this over to the Hartes' house."

The young girl blinked. "Right now, Miss Samantha? I haven't touched the silver yet, and it's in frightful need of polish."

"Yes, right now. And Daisy, you are to give it to no one except Charlotte. No one else is to see this note, do you understand?"

"Yes ma'am, I'll set to it right now."

With that, as soon as Daisy left, Samantha almost jumped on the bed with the joy she felt. Soon she and her beloved Charlotte would be on their way. After four long years of planning, dreaming, it was finally going to happen.

No longer prisoner to corsets. To feminine frills and coquettish pretense. Samantha felt absolutely giddy as she lay back on the bed the afternoon sunlight beaming in through the window warming her all over. She grabbed a pillow, hugged it close, and then closed her eyes. Dreaming that it was Charlotte in her arms.

She woke with a start as she heard a knock. She sat up, saw that the failing light of the evening had been replaced by the rising sun.

"Miss Samantha," Daisy called, "Are you ready to change for breakfast?"

"Yes, I am," she replied, as she rubbed sleep sand from her eyes. "Daisy, come in. I must have fallen asleep after you left."

Daisy entered, her kind face lit up with a brilliant smile. Samantha felt with a pang that Daisy was the one person she was going to miss from this house.

Samantha couldn't contain her excitement at the maid's expression.

"Did you give my note to Miss Harte?"

"Yes, ma'am, I did. She read it and said she'll be visiting within the hour."

"Wonderful! Now I have something good to focus on while you help me change."

Giddy with the good news, Samantha slipped out of the dress she had hastily donned earlier the evening before.

"Oh!" Daisy giggled, "Miss Samantha, you ain't got no underthings on. Do you want me to get your corset?'

"No thank you! I'll never wear one of those things again, if I have my way about it."

Daisy let out a helpless sigh.

She proceeded to help dress her mistress as fashionably as she could, even without the corset to enhance her feminine charms. Once properly attired, Samantha descended to the dining room once again.

Percy had vanished from the scene, but the gleeful look on her father's face chilled her in a way that the man's anger could not. Good fortune for McKinley Williams more often than not meant bad fortune for his daughter.

Samantha took her seat, nerves jangling as her father took a trio of hearty puffs at his first cigar of the morning.

"You're tardy," he pronounced, with bluff good cheer. "And when I have such excellent news for you, too!"

"And what good news might that be?"

"It's about Percy Hanover," he said, with a smile full of shark's teeth. "He has asked for your hand in marriage."

CHAPTER 3

Samantha's eyes burned into her father's face like a pair of hot coals.

"He asked you for my hand in marriage," she repeated slowly. "And you of course refused?"

"Don't be impertinent! He is a good catch, and you know it." Almost as an afterthought, he added, "The wedding will be in two weeks."

She tamped down the urge to scream bloody murder at her father. He sat there, so smug and secure. Auctioning her off like a prize heifer.

"Why was I not consulted in the matter of my own marriage?"

McKinley shrugged. "I hardly need to consult you to make a decision concerning your welfare."

Thoughts ran wild in her head, like telegraph lines spitting out streams of Morse code.

I won't be here anyway, so it doesn't matter. Pay no mind.

But act normal! Don't be too complacent. He'll think something is amiss.

"You mean *your* welfare, don't you?" she said, in an icy tone. "Percy's your age. Why on earth would I want to marry him?"

"The decision has been made, girl! I will be making the arrangements tomorrow, so you had better get used to the idea."

"So I have no choice in the matter?"

"No, you don't. And there is one more thing," he said, shaking a finger at his daughter, "I don't want to catch you riding again, not before your wedding! After that, I don't care. You and your unseemly ways will be Percy's problem."

Daisy approached the table, tentatively whenever in the presence of Samantha's father. More than once, she'd fainted dead away from a blast of McKinley's gruff temper.

"Mister Williams, it's Miss Harte, here to see Miss Samantha."

"Father," Samantha said, hiding her eagerness, "May I go tell her the news?"

"By all means, go ahead." He dismissed her with an out of hand gesture and picked up his fork and knife as the cook set out a golden, runny mound of fried eggs and a slab of steak before him. "I'm sure that you girls will have all sort of plans to make."

"You are so right, Father," Samantha said, with a smile. "We girls do have lots of plans to make."

* * *

Charlotte Harte looked every inch the properly dressed debutante as she stood at the parlor window, watching hummingbirds sip nectar from a patch of foxglove. Dressed in mint green chiffon, with a straw bonnet festooned with ribbons and silk flowers set upon her russet curls, she looked as fresh and verdant as a spring day.

Samantha caught her breath as she came into the parlor and saw the young woman standing there, aglow in a shaft of warm spring sunlight.

"Oh, Char," she said, "I'm so glad you're here."

Charlotte took Samantha's hands in hers and led her to the window seat. They sat down and embraced, careful, always careful not to show too much affection in public. But Samantha knew better. Behind closed doors, Charlotte would nuzzle and rub up against her like a tigress in heat!

"Samantha," Charlotte breathed. The southern belle's delicate voice trilled with a drawl that sent warm shivers down Samantha's spine. "I got your note, but I want to know – what in the world's gotten your dander up so?"

"We have to leave as soon as possible. My father gave me to Percy Hanover for marriage."

"What?" Charlotte sputtered. "That...that fat old man? Why, he's your daddy's age, and stinks of cee-gars. What's your father thinkin'? Oh, it makes me ill. I am ever so sorry for you!"

"Yes. That fat old man. So you see, we *have* to leave. It's not like we can wait anymore."

"Well, I see, but..."

"It's not like we haven't been planning on this before! Everything's already laid out, all we have to do is put it into action."

Charlotte pulled back, her doe eyes wide and filled with surprise.

"But Samantha, honey...that was only play actin'. Weren't it? We were just pretending...weren't we?"

Disbelief crept onto Samantha face.

"No, it wasn't, and we weren't! I meant everything I said. And now is the time. The wedding date's been set. Two weeks from now."

Charlotte wrung her hands. She turned toward the garden, away from Samantha's pleading eyes.

"I...I don't know..."

Samantha fought to control her emotions once more. She brought her voice down to a whisper full of reproach.

"I thought you loved me."

"I do love you! It's just..."

"Just what?"

"I need some time to think on it. My momma would be plumb devastated if I just up an' lit out with you. And my daddy? Why, my daddy would disown me, sure as the sun comes up tomorrow."

Samantha stared in disbelief. She stood up and her voice trembled as she spoke. "I will leave day after tomorrow at daybreak. With or without you."

"Samantha, please—"

"No," Samantha shook her head. "You need to make up your mind, Charlotte Harte. And you need to make it up before tomorrow night."

Charlotte sat as if rooted to the spot. Her eyes never left Samantha's face.

"If you decide that you want to be with me," Samantha continued, "I'll meet you just outside of town. By the old bridge at Parker's Slough."

Charlotte's voice trembled. "Do you know what you're askin' me to do?"

"Yes." She reached down and caressed Charlotte's cheek. "But I'll hope that you find enough courage in your heart. Enough love in there. Enough to leave this behind and come with me."

Beyond caring if anyone saw, Samantha drew Charlotte's face up towards hers. She tenderly touched her lips to Charlotte's, as tears began to fall from her eyes.

Charlotte's eyes closed. She shivered with the intensity of the kiss that passed between the two women.

But she didn't say another word.

With a choked sob, Samantha turned and ran from the room.

CHAPTER 4

Samantha spent much of the morning packing everything she could possibly think she'd need in a pair of saddlebags. It turned out to be easier than she'd anticipated. No room for delicate frippery or taffeta dresses anymore.

She needed heavy trousers, work shirts, clothes that could withstand travel and heavy wear from saddle leather and the elements. She fished out her muddy riding boots, cleaned them lovingly, and then stashed them and the full-to-bursting saddlebags back under her bed. Just in case her father – or, God forbid, Percy Hanover – were to make an appearance.

Through Daisy, she smuggled up to her room a small assortment of pans and cutlery. And she was able to send orders to have her horse, Jubilee, to be put in the stall and given an extra ration of oats for the night.

Dinnertime came and went. Samantha knew that she should eat, but her stomach played host to a whole flock of butterflies. Once done with the chore of packing, her mind ran riot, thinking about Charlotte's answer.

The months of planning for this day…were they truly just a game to her? Surely Charlotte knew how Samantha felt! Until that morning, she'd been so sure that Charlotte had felt the same way. The two of them, against the entire world.

Could it be that tomorrow, she was fated to be totally on her own? Forever? Samantha rubbed her eyes with the heels of her hands and sank back on her bed as the darkness of the night finally fell. With those evil thoughts rumbling through her brain, she fell into an uneasy sleep.

She woke to the glow of a candle and a whisper at the side of her bed.

"Miss Samantha?"

"Daisy!" she whispered in return. "What is it?"

"If you're set on leaving, dawn's an hour away," Daisy said quietly. "And I made sure that your father got his full bottle of brandy last night. He's three sheets to the wind and not going to be stirring, 'less you drop an anvil on his pate."

Samantha threw her arms around her maid, stifling a cry of joy and a sob. Tousling the girl's hair, she spoke with true affection in her voice.

"Thank you, Daisy. I'll never forget you."

"You've always been kind to me, Miss Samantha. I'll miss you something awful too."

And with that, Samantha slipped out of her feminine house wear and into her riding gear. She grasped the saddlebags in one hand, the cooking gear in the other. Though the pots clanged and rattled as she went down the stairs, the sound had nothing on the seismic rumble of her father's alcohol-induced snoring.

The morning air hung heavy with a damp chill as Samantha hurried to the stables. Smell of horse manure, tingle of wood fires burning in distant hearths. And yet, under these scents lay something exhilarating. Subtle, like morning dew, like fresh-bloomed honeysuckle, like new-mown hay.

Samantha knew what it was, as soon as she tacked up Jubilee and swung herself into the saddle.

Freedom.

Calling her, drawing her like a moth to a lantern's wick, pulling her to the west. Dawn peeked over her left shoulder as Jubilee trotted down Chicago's cobblestoned street, heading for the outskirts of town.

Mist continued to collect in goose-pimpling droplets against Samantha's eyelashes and forearms as she rode on. The early morning sun, rather than burning off the fog, simply turned it pinker, harder to see through. Around her, the houses gradually diminished in size. Open lots and fields began to appear. And up ahead, the road reared up over a marshy stream into a small stone arch.

Someone mounted atop a small brown-and-white paint horse waited by the old bridge. The figure wore a man's denim jacket, a riding cap, and trousers. The animal's white spots reflected the morning light and gave a mottled, almost camouflaged look to whoever sat in the saddle.

A harsh whisper echoed in the fog bank as the figure leaned forward, as if squinting.

"Sam? Is that you?"

Samantha's heart gave a lurch and for a moment she held her breath. Almost afraid to believe that Charlotte waited for her.

"Char?"

"'Course it is! Who else would be fool enough to go riding on a godforsaken mornin' like this?"

Samantha's horse ambled over and came nose to nose with Charlotte's little paint steed, Patches. The two young women dismounted, then came together and embraced.

Charlotte pulled gently away from Samantha. Her breathing sounded harsh, on the edge of panic.

"We better get a movin' on. I'm sure that we'll be missed soon, and I...well, I might lose my nerve."

"Yes, we had better get going," Samantha agreed, as they remounted. She indicated the heavier, masculine clothing they both wore. "Though I don't think anyone would recognize us in this get up."

"I thought as much," Charlotte admitted, as they nudged their horses into a trot. "It's stiff, this outfit. Got it as a parting gift from our old Aussie stable hand."

"You got yours from Quincy?" Samantha shook her head in amazement. "I bought mine, but only when he had time to go to the shop with me, show me what I needed, how to use it."

"Sounds like what he taught us might well come in handy," Charlotte said, "Never thought I'd use any of his teachings this way...but I'm not findin' that I mind it especially much."

A burst of warmth settled in Samantha's heart as the two emerged from the fog and headed west. They kept a steady pace, anxious to put distance between them and the town's outermost limits.

The sun finally decided to burn away the fog. But what they gained in visibility, they paid for in heat and glare. A few hours into their ride, and Charlotte reeled in her saddle. Samantha spurred Jubilee up to Patches' side and steadied her with a hand to the shoulder.

"Sam," Charlotte said wearily, "Can we stop a moment? I am plum tuckered out, and my stomach done thinks my throat's been cut."

Samantha saw the stress and strain on her companion's face. Charlotte simply wasn't accustomed to long hours of riding. Especially not astride like a man. She nodded towards a wooded glen, just off the road.

"Sure, let's head over there."

Sunlight through birch and elm branches dappled the two as they stopped their horses and dismounted. Charlotte's legs almost gave way as she dismounted, and her thighs fairly burned with soreness from the ride, and the rough cloth that made up the men's trousers.

"I don't know how on earth you stand this," Charlotte waddled in a stiff, bowlegged gait over to a rock sitting on the edge of the pool.

Samantha laughed. "Trust me, you'll get used to it."

She unsaddled the horses and put hobbles on them so that they could graze without wandering too far. Samantha untied a rucksack that hung from her saddle, pulled out hunks of bread and cheese, and then handed them to Charlotte. In a rather unladylike fashion, Charlotte took a big bite of one, then the other, stuffing her mouth till her cheeks bulged.

Samantha laughed merrily and pulled out a second helping for herself. She shared out a canteen of water with Charlotte.

Though fresh, the liquid had already taken on a metallic flavor. Charlotte grimaced at the taste.

"Sorry," Samantha said. "Until we get out to the wilderness proper, we're not bound to find water fresh enough to drink right from a stream."

Charlotte shook her head in amazement. "I don't rightly know which I'd find more troublesome right now — wading into an ice-cold stream for water, or gettin' atop Patches. My legs haven't decided that they can come back together."

"Yeah, I know. But we need to put a few more miles on before it gets dark. I'll bet our fathers will be keen to put someone on our trail in no time."

"You're right." Charlotte said ruefully, as she creakily got up and took her hat off for the first time that morning. Samantha started as she saw that Charlotte had cut her russet-colored tresses all off, leaving a short fringe of curls about her face. "Got any ideas as to where we're headed, in the end?"

"We're following the sun. We'll know when we get there."

Charlotte stared at her for a moment. "I like poetry, but it don't sit well with me right now. Samantha honey, are y'all sure about this?"

Samantha looked back with serious determination in her eyes.

"I won't go back. Not to that life. Not *ever!*"

Charlotte said nothing in reply. But Samantha couldn't help but feel a chill steal over her heart as her lover's cherubic face took on a sullen, crestfallen look.

CHAPTER 5

McKinley Williams flung his morning's coffee, mug and all, as hard as he could across the room. An explosion of crockery and sweet-smelling steam. Richly scented drops of Arabia's best dripped down the imported wallpaper, staining it as if the house itself had become diseased.

His voice boomed out in irritation. "What do you mean, 'she's vanished'?"

"It just that, Mister McKinley!" Daisy shrunk away from him. "I looked for Miss Samantha in her room, in the stable. Jubilee, her horse, he's gone too."

"Get out," he rumbled, and then raised his voice to a shout. *"Get out!"*

Daisy dashed out of the room as if expecting another volley of china and coffee to follow.

McKinley slumped in his chair just as the butler entered and timidly faced his employer.

"Sir, Mr. and Mrs. Harte are here to see you. On an urgent matter."

"What in blue blazes do they want, Tom?"

"I would suggest that you speak with them yourself, sir."

"Don't be impertinent!"

The door to the parlor swung open with a *bang*. Tom stepped adroitly aside as Charlotte's parents, both as pale skinned and russet-haired as a matched pair of porcelain dolls, burst into the room. Charlotte's mother shook as if in a high fever. Tears streamed from her red, puffy eyes. Her father's voice, tinged with the same hint of Dixie as his daughter's, rung in McKinley's ears.

"She's gone!" he shouted, "My dear baby Charlotte, she's gone!"

Mrs. Harte let out a wail in counterpoint. McKinley Williams stared at the couple for a moment, his earlier outburst forgotten. He knew Mary Harte from the elaborate garden parties she'd thrown for her own daughter, Charlotte. And he knew Nathaniel Harte from the Chamber of Commerce and a couple gentlemanly games of whist.

Neither had struck him as prone to hysterics.

"What are you looking at me for, Nathaniel? Why don't you go to the police?"

"Because I'm certain that your family's got somethin' to do with this." Nathaniel Harte drew himself up, tugged at the ends of his jacket, and jabbed a gloved finger in McKinley's face. "It was your daughter, McKinley! Your daughter who kept dragging ours to those damned equestrian events, kept her out late nights, and got her into who-knows-what mischief."

McKinley Williams stared at the man. A deep suspicion began to grow in the back of his mind, but he kept it tamped down for now.

"My daughter's gone missing too," he grated. Charlotte's mother stopped in mid-sniffle to listen as Samantha's father called over to the butler. "Tom, get me the Pinkerton Detective Agency, right away. Have them send me their best man."

Two hours crawled by. Hours made all the longer by Mrs. Harte's near-constant crying. Suddenly, a solid-sounding rap from the entryway's brass knocker. All eyes followed the butler as he went to the door.

McKinley fought to control his fidgeting as he heard the muffled sounds of talking and steps inside the front hall. Last night, he'd thought his fortune had been made. When Percy Hanover all but drooled over Samantha. Then asked for her hand in marriage. At last his goal had become within reach. The prestige he so justly deserved!

And now this.

Well, he wouldn't stand for it. No, he would get her back, at any cost. She would not upset his plans.

Tom returned to the parlor, announcing solemnly, "Sir, Matthew Slade of the Pinkerton Agency is here to see you."

Mrs. Harte remained seated while Nathaniel and McKinley rose to greet the new arrival. The Pinkerton man stood a full head taller than either of them. A smart tweed suit outlined his tall, lean frame, and his strong hand held a dapper bowler hat by a worn brim. His waxed handlebar mustache, smelling pleasantly of barbershop cologne, preceded his strong handshake as he greeted everyone in turn.

"Well Mister Williams," Slade said grandly, in a voice one part Western drawl, one part smooth Tennessee whiskey. "What can Pinkerton do for you?"

"Hopefully, a great deal," McKinley stated. In a matter-of-fact tone, he added, "Our daughters have been kidnapped."

At his statement, Mary Harte let out a blubbering sob and fainted dead away in her chair. Nathaniel went to her side as McKinley looked on with annoyance.

"Tom," he called, "Bring us some smelling salts. Any more of this nonsense and I might go into feminine hysterics too."

Matthew Slade pinched one end of his mustache in his fingers as he looked on in calculation and amusement. However, his tone dropped a shade as he grew deadly serious.

"Mister Williams, what makes you think that your daughter Samantha has been kidnapped?"

"Why else would she just disappear with her wedding so close?"

"Oh?" One eyebrow rose. "She's gettin' married?"

"As a matter of fact, she is. To Percy Hanover, of the Lake Forest—"

"I'm aware of them. Quite a rich family. Percy's been born with an entire drawer of silver spoons in his mouth. All the more strange."

McKinley frowned. "How do you mean?"

"A kidnapper should've waited by-the-by. Taking the blushing bride of a man like Percy Hanover would've reaped a tidier sum. Was there a ransom note?"

"Well, ah, no. No note was found."

The butler arrived, with Daisy and her vial of smelling salts in tow. She attended to Mary Harte as Nathaniel turned his attention to focus on Slade.

"I understand that the Harte girl has gone missing also? Is that correct?"

Harte nodded. "Yes, that's quite right. Charlotte's gone."

"Any ransom note?" Harte nodded again, this time in the negative.

"Does it not seem a bit odd that both of your daughters have gone missing at the same time? And that no ransom note was left for either one?"

"Hellfire, man!" McKinley burst out. "What else do you need to know? They're missing. We want them back, and you're wasting time!"

Slade gave the man a non-plussed look.

"Mister McKinley, I've been the lead investigator for some sixty cases for Pinkerton. In that time, I've never failed to close one. That's because I knew exactly what I was getting into from the start, each time."

Matthew Slade looked each man in the eye as he spoke. He drew himself to his full height and made his next statement in a tone that brooked no disagreement.

"So, gentlemen. How about each of you tellin' me what's *really* going on here?"

CHAPTER 6

McKinley Williams clamped his jaw tight as if a steel trap had snapped shut on it. When no answer was forthcoming, Slade let out a tired sigh and spoke again.

"Mister Williams," Slade said, "How did your daughter feel about getting hitched to Percy Hanover?"

As if against his will, McKinley said, "Elated, of course. The man's from one of the oldest and wealthiest families in Chicago."

"I'm also aware that he's a man of your age. And your daughter is...what? Nineteen or twenty? Sir, it's very important that you be honest with me. I am askin' you again. Did Samantha want this marriage?"

McKinley Williams grabbed his jacket lapels in both hands. "What does that matter? I'm her father, and she'll do as I say. It's no business is it of yours, anyway. If you can't find her and bring her back, then I'll hire someone who will."

Slade ignored the last of McKinley's statements. Instead, he turned to Nathaniel. "Mister Harte, Charlotte's horse is missing, I expect?"

"You're correct," Harte said, surprised. "How did you know that?"

"Because I passed the stable on the way in." Slade held up a hand to forestall McKinley's reaction. "One whole side's laid out for a female rider, from the type of tack on the shelves to the height they're laid out at. And though there's no sign of struggle, the stall hasn't been mucked out yet."

"What're you implying, Slade?"

"I'm not much for 'implying', Mister Harte." Slade shrugged. "I'm a simple man who just calls it as he sees it. Like I said, no sign of a struggle. And muckin' a stall is a morning task. It all adds up to one thing: Samantha Williams took her horse out on her own, before anyone was awake. No one kidnapped your daughters. They left on their own."

"But why would Charlotte leave?" Harte threw Williams a dark look. "We've tried to encourage her to see some boys. She hasn't been excited about that...but she wasn't about to be pressured into no marriage."

McKinley's uneasy look attracted Slade's eye. "Is there something that you want to tell me, Mister Williams?"

"There may be a reason for that. My daughter is good friends with Charlotte. And Samantha has...un-natural tendencies."

"What do you mean? Un-natural tendencies?"

"She prefers the company of women rather than men."

This time it was Mary Harte who jumped to her feet, pushing away the maid's and butler's ministrations.

"Not my Charlotte," she said. "She's a chaste and proper young woman!"

"Oh, please!" McKinley snapped. "She's as much a Sapphist as Samantha. I've seen them returning late at night, trading kisses that were anything but sisterly."

"Why didn't you tell us?"

"Because they just need a good man, Mary. Marriage and children will take care of that nonsense!" McKinley turned to glare at Slade. "So now you know. These two may not want to be found. I don't care. I will not have my plans for my daughter thwarted by some silly nonsense."

Slade ran a finger along one side of his mustache in thought. Nodding to himself, he fixed his steely gray eyes on the two men.

"I'll take this case," he pronounced. "Mister Williams, your daughter is a very resourceful young lady. That said, I don't

113

think they're going to blaze a trail into the Great White North or out west into Indian country."

Mary Harte let out a gasp at that, but Nathaniel steadied her, while adding, "Charlotte's got a bunch of relations down south. Georgia, mostly."

"And the branches of my family are in Pennsylvania and Boston," McKinley said. "It's possible that they hopped a train back to Philadelphia."

Slade nodded. "I'll have a telegraph sent to all Pinkerton branches within a day's train ride from Chicago to watch the rail stations. Myself, I'll get to trailing them as soon as I get my gear together."

Nathaniel Harte looked up at Slade with a haggard expression. "I just want to know what's happened to my daughter. If she's gone off on her own, I want to know, and I want to know why. Please Mister Slade, please find her."

"Count on it," Slade said firmly. "There's a reason I was picked to run the Chicago branch of Pinkerton's. I've never failed to bring in my man."

Slade excused himself and left the room. He stopped by the front door and carefully placed his bowler hat back on his head. The butler graciously opened the door with a slight bow.

"Tell me something, Tom." Slade tilted his head, indicating the parlor. "Is Mister Williams always this pleasant?"

"Sir, one never speaks ill of their employer. To do so would lead to short term employment."

"Thank you, Tom. You just told me what I wanted to know."

"Quite right, sir."

Matthew Slade stepped out into the bright, cool morning. The air echoed with the busy *clack-clack* of horses' hooves and drawn carriage wheels on cobblestone streets. He looked back up at the Williams' house. The sound of muffled, heated conversation came from the leaded glass of the parlor window.

Slade grimaced, and then raised the brim of his hat to look further up the side of the house. His gaze roved over the dark red of the clinker-brick siding, a spray of ivy, and rested on the black metal weather vane that perched atop the roof. The vane's arrow swung uneasily in the slight breeze, indicating no certain direction.

He shook his head. *How very fitting.*

* * *

The sun had sunk low on the horizon when Samantha turned to see Charlotte trailing behind her. Her companion looked as tired and bedraggled as her horse.

"Char," she called, "How about we find a place to camp for the night?"

For the first time in what seemed like hours, Charlotte's eyes lit up and a smile crept across her face.

"You mean it? My fanny seems to've *growed* to this saddle."

Samantha made sure not to laugh at Charlotte's discomfort. She'd had more than a few days like that when she first started riding.

"Of course I mean it." Samantha pointed to a tall bluff up ahead, one with a slight overhang. As best as she could see, the place would give them a little extra shelter. The tall trees stood dense and close enough for a tether line for the horses.

"Well, so long as I can just get down offen' this horse."

Samantha dismounted, then helped Charlotte all but slide down the side of the saddle. Her companion hunched over stiffly, as if she'd aged thirty years in the last eight hours.

"God in heaven, I won't be able to put my legs back together ever again."

Samantha picked up Patches' reins and nodded towards the base of the bluff. "You go on over there and sit a spell. I'll take care of the horses."

Charlotte limped over to sit on a fallen log. She almost collapsed onto the ground with a howl as the rough fabric of her trousers rubbed against her chaffed legs. Samantha did her best to pay no mind to the noise as she removed their mounts' bridles and replaced them with halters and lead lines, tying them next to each other.

After removing the saddles, she gave the horses a rub down with the saddle blankets. Next, she put the feed bags over their heads with the ration of grain she'd thought to bring along. Having taken care of the horses, Samantha brought the saddlebags over to where Charlotte sat, rubbing her thighs and groaning.

"It's getting dark," Samantha said. "I'd better get us a fire going."

No comment from Charlotte.

Samantha gathered some rocks and put them in a circle. She gathered dry twigs and pieces of bracken piling it up into a heap in the middle, thankful that she had brought a lot of matches with her, as the fire took six tries before catching.

She jumped as the sky opened with a peal of thunder. The smell of rain hung heavy in the air for a moment. The first drops of rain started to fall, causing the fire to sputter and pop.

The *plinks* of water on the fire matched the first tears from Charlotte's eyes. Before Samantha could think of anything to say, to ask what was wrong, more tears streamed down Charlotte's cheeks.

Charlotte buried her head in her hands and began to sob.

CHAPTER 7

Samantha rushed to Charlotte's side.

"Char! What's the matter?"

"What do you think's the matter?" Charlotte flared at her. "I'm tired. Hungry. I hurt all over. I've been dropped down smack the middle of God knows where and now it's *raining!*"

Not knowing what else to do, Samantha pulled a heavy woolen blanket from the bedroll pack and wrapped it around the two of them. Samantha held Charlotte close, using her body heat to warm her as she stroked the soft curls of hair and rocked her gently.

"I know you're tired and all." A pause, as Samantha held her tighter. "But it'll get better, I promise."

Samantha drew back her head and raised her hands to take Charlotte's face in them, leaned forward and kissed the tear stained cheeks. Charlotte looked back at her. Doubt simmered in her eyes.

"Right now, I want you to just sit here while I get us some supper. I got us some fine canned beans here that'll fix you right up. Thank goodness this cliff hangs out enough to protect the fire from the rain."

On cue, the fire sputtered as a burst of lightening and a loud thunderclap exploded over their heads.

Somehow, the fire kept going and a grateful Samantha opened a can of beans and heated them in the same can. She held a spoon toward Charlotte and coaxed her to eat them.

Samantha then broke out a saucepan, heated water in it to a boil, and added coffee to the bubbling liquid. To Samantha, the rising fumes smelled heavenly. But even so, between the bland food, the bitter taste of the coffee, and the sandy grit of the grounds, Charlotte couldn't do more than finish half of what Samantha put out for her.

The rain began to slacken off, but a chilling wind kicked up. Charlotte just stared dully into the distance, until she finally broke her silence.

"I want to go home."

Samantha looked down at her hands. "You know I can't ever do that. You know what waits for me there."

"I know. But I do ever so want to go home. To be home again..." Charlotte's voice wound down, and she went quiet again. Samantha could feel the silence weighing down on them like a sodden tarp.

She left her companion to make sure the horses were alright and secure for the night. When she came back Charlotte had fallen asleep, huddled up like a little girl. The rain finally stopped. Samantha fed a long brand into the fire as it burned, and then sat down and stretched her hands out to warm them. She realized for the first time since they had arrived at the campsite how tired she really felt.

From where she sat she could see the black sky, like a piece of fine velvet studded and spangled with diamonds. It reminded her of a dress her mother had worn at one of the parties given to impress her father's so-called friends.

The thought made her shudder.

No, I'll never go back.

Unable to sleep, not knowing what the next day would bring. Not knowing if it had been wise to ask Charlotte to go with her. Wondering if her love for Charlotte would be enough of a bond.

Knowing in her heart that she would go through hell's fire rather than going back to her father's tyranny. Before she'd be forced into a man's bed. And as sleep finally stole upon her, Samantha realized that she just might have to face the devil himself.

Alone.

* * *

McKinley Williams watched with gimlet eyes as the Pinkerton detective patted the sturdy-looking roan mustang. The man then slipped his Winchester into the scabbard on his mount's rig. Matthew Slade was almost unrecognizable in the leather britches, the silver concho'd vest and the low slung Colt. A gunfighter's rig, except for the tie downs left loose for riding.

"Slade, I demand to know why you're heading out on horseback," McKinley said loftily, "You should be looking for clues to where my daughter has gone, down at the train station!"

Slade tamped down the response that first came to mind before he spoke. "Mister Williams, rule number one when you hire my firm: don't tell a Pinkerton man how to run his case."

He paused, letting McKinley stew before he went on.

"My men are covering train stations and the telegraph posts in a four-hundred mile radius from Chicago. I'll be in touch with them, they'll be giving me reports. I'll be passing on what I hear to you as I see fit."

"Second, it don't take a genius to see that, unless they're desperate, those two ain't going to be taking the trains. Samantha at least knows that you'd be hiring someone like me. They'll stick to horseback. And so will I."

"Well, they can't have gone far," McKinley declared. "At least, not so that nobody would notice."

"That's the first thing you've been right about, so far," Slade said. McKinley blinked, unsure whether to be insulted or not.

"It is?"

"Yup. On horseback, the roads are good down south to Saint Louie, or back east to Toledo. Good, and busy. I should be able to find out in a couple of days if anyone's seen them."

"That should be the end of it, then."

"That's not what my gut says, no," Slade said, as he put his foot up into the stirrup and swung his lanky frame up and into the saddle. "Going south or east, that's the right thing to do, if they're seeking help from a relative. But...what if they're not doing that? Where would they go, if they decided that they'd be puttin' it all on one throw?"

McKinley bristled. "I'm not in the habit of visiting gambling halls, so I don't understand your 'colorful' way of speaking. These are just two girls, Slade. What could they possibly do that's unexpected?"

"What indeed?" Slade replied quietly. He tipped his hat to McKinley Williams, and then nudged the mustang into a trot. The horse's hooves threw up dirt clods that sprayed the man's trousers, causing him to jump back and curse.

Slade chuckled to himself. He didn't like McKinley, or any man like him. It got to him, being on a case he didn't like. Samantha had no choice but to run from her father and a repulsive arranged marriage. He wasn't sure about Charlotte, but anyone willing to cut loose the way she did...it could only mean one thing.

Love.

Slade couldn't blame either of them. A lot at stake. A shame he had to get this job. The two young women didn't stand a chance.

"Git up." Slade nudged the mustang to a fast lope as they headed out of Chicago and into the vast open spaces of the West.

To read the rest of *Sagebrush and Lace*,
please visit your favorite online bookseller
for the eBook or Print edition.

MEET DEVLIN CHURCH
& MICHAEL ANGEL

Devlin Church was born to a pair of Wild West rodeo show performers who later became regulars with a traveling circus. Since someone decided it would be useful for her to know how to read and write, she ended up at Catholic boarding school. It was an equitable trade—the nuns gave her literacy, and she gave them heartburn with her rebellious ways.

She has worked as a Technical Writer, a hypnotherapist, Continuous Improvement Manager, and artist. She's tried her hand at corporate management, three children, and as many marriages.

Connect with Devlin Church online at:
http://www.glair.biz

Michael Angel is a professional writer whose books have been published internationally by mainstream 'dead tree' publishers in Italian, Portuguese, French, Dutch, Korean, German, Russian, and Chinese.

One of his nonfiction books was selected as a textbook for upper division biology courses in the California public university system. Nothing thrills him more than to know that somewhere, right now, there are bright young people who are *required* to read his work.

He currently resides in Southern California.

Connect with Michael Angel online at:
http://tinyurl.com/MichaelAngelWriter
http://tinyurl.com/michaelangel-facebook

Made in the USA
Charleston, SC
05 March 2013